Ron Butlin was born in 1949 in ... variously as a footman, a male mod... Thames barges, he has become o... writers of his generation. His works include the nov... of My Voice and Night Visits, and a collection of stories, The Tilting Room, as well as four books of poetry and several radio plays. He won the Scottish Arts Council Award 2003 for work-in-progress, which included Vivaldi and the Number 3.

**Praise for two earlier titles by Ron Butlin
published by Serpent's Tail**

The Sound of My Voice

'One of the greatest pieces of fiction to come out of Britain in the '80s...Butlin's book is a stylistic triumph...I anticipate that *The Sound of My Voice* will receive the recognition it deserves as a major novel' Irvine Welsh

'One of the most inventive and daring novels ever to have come out of Scotland. Ron Butlin is that rarest of breeds — a poet who takes the novel form and shows that it is ripe for reinvention. Playful, haunting and moving, this is writing of the highest quality' Ian Rankin

'A stylistic masterpiece...Chilling but extremely enjoyable' *Daily Mail*

'Compulsively readable...a cleverly orchestrated, unique work of fiction' *Glasgow Herald*

'Written with extraordinary economy and use of internal echo' *The Scotsman*

'A powerful portrait of alcoholism and self-destruction' *Bookseller Paperback Preview*

'An extraordinarily powerful and redemptive work, as impressive for its use of language as for its emotional appeal' Nicholas Royle, *Time Out*

'Haunting, dark, relentless' *Uncut*

'Brutal and bruising, this is as near to the edge as you can get without falling. Totally recommended' *Crack*

Night Visits

'Like his landmark *The Sound of My Voice*, Ron Butlin's *Night Visits* creates a displaced world of jeopardy and emotional damage' Alan Warner

'Butlin writes with penetrating insight and reassuring compassion about people who have exhausted their own supplies of hope, yet in his hands they are never entirely hopeless' *Time Out*

'Beautifully structured...Butlin empathises as well as any writer dealing with the pain of adolescent trauma I've read...What makes the achievement special, however, is the way in which warped adolescent yearning is interwoven with a very different and repressed yearning, that of Malcolm's Aunt Fiona [who is] an archetype of inner corrosion and suffering...Butlin handles the delicate savagery of her condition with a rare combination of sympathy and detachment, and its climax...is as fine in its portrayal of psychological destruction and reconstruction as *The Sound of My Voice*' *Books in Scotland*

'Sick, disturbing, menacing, exceptionally good...Excellently depicted and a credit to the skill and compassion of Butlin, this is contemporary fiction at its classic best' *The Void*

'This Bergman-bleak novel is devastating but eventually uplifting. Marvellous' *Uncut*

'Butlin's crisp prose oscillates between the real and the surreal, providing the perfect poetic metaphor for this powerful portrait of corrosion and pain' *The Herald* (Glasgow)

'Though the setting lends itself to gothic overstatement, Butlin's exploration of emotional abuse is shocking without being sensationalist' *Guardian*

Vivaldi and the number 3

and other impossible stories

Ron Butlin

Illustrations by John Sibbald

SERPENT'S TAIL

Library of Congress Catalog Card Number: 2004103022

A complete catalogue record for this book can be obtained
from the British Library on request

The right of Ron Butlin to be identified as the author of this
work has been asserted by him in accordance with the
Copyright, Designs and Patents Act 1988

Copyright © 2004 by Ron Butlin

First published in 2004 by Serpent's Tail,
4 Blackstock Mews, London N4 2BT
website: www.serpentstail.com

Typeset at Neuadd Bwll, Llanwrtyd Wells

Printed by Mackays of Chatham, plc
10   9   8   7   6   5   4   3   2   1

This book is for my wife Regi, for my friends in music: Iain Bamforth, Jonathan Barker, León Coates, Lyell Cresswell, Ken Dempster, Andrew Greig, Ed Harper, Peter Porter, Julia Schwartz, Martin Staub, Alex Storm; Jamie Thomson; and for those who play among the carry-out troughs and wine bottles at Schubertiads, listen-iads and vin-iads: Mark Bailey, Phil Burrin, Graham Cumberland and Roger Quin.

Contents

Acknowledgements   xi

The lives

Vivaldi, the jumping cardinal, God and the number 3   3
Vivaldi and the heavens' multicoloured luminous stars   9
Vivaldi learns a new skill   17
Alma Mahler leaves the nineteenth century behind   21
How Bach won the battle against modern technology   29
Beethoven's response to the hanging gardens of neglect   33
Johannes Brahms goes in search of his first symphony   41
The fairy-tale science-fiction world of Antonin Dvořák   49
Haydn learns to put his demon to good use   57
Mozart tries out a major career move   65
Schubert and the magic business card   71
Travelling via San Francisco and the moon:
             seven days in the life of Robert Schumann   81
Jean Sibelius is invited to run away and join the circus   89
Richard Strauss and Pharaoh Amenhotep IV – their dreams   95
Tchaikovsky decides which world he belongs to   107
Tafelmusik and cat-scarers: a brief biography of
             the real Georg Telemann   111
The Mighty Handful versus the rest of the world   121

The letters

How Composer Q chose a better life   131
Girls, glamour and real estate: the secret life of Composer X   139
How recent, irreversible changes in the world have
                    affected the life of Composer Y   145
Composer Z explores the emptiness lying beyond
                    the end of the alphabet   149

The thoughts

David Hume and the pixels of gratification   157
Nietzsche breaks through the cycle of eternal recurrence   163
Seneca comes to the Southside   169
Socrates celebrates the opening of the first supermarket   177

The last word

Nadia Boulanger has the last word   185

Notes about the composers and philosophers   193

Illustrations

He draws strength from the wingèd
        cherubim and seraphim   xii

The aerodynamically designed wellingtons
        to reduce surface tension   19

'You bastard!' She wrote it out again. This time
        sustaining the B flat, just to be sure   23

The desert reverberated to their salaam of awe
        in the revealed face of their Godhead   99

He was holding something to his ear, shaking it   119

Pouf! The magnesium flare lit up the huddle of players,
        their ice-stiffened beards and chilled knees   124

He's paused for her to ask who Linnaeus was   153

Murray edged forward into the kitchen:
        'Have I called at a bad time?'   173

Acknowledgements

Some of these stories first appeared in *Ambit, The Barcelona Review, Cencrastus, Chapman, Edinburgh Review, Northwords, Product, riverrun, Endangered Species* –the Arts Council's Online Anthology, *The Scottish Book Collector*; several have been broadcast on BBC Radio 4.

I would like to thank the Scottish Arts Council for a Writers' Bursary which allowed me time to complete this book.

Thanks also to Felix for keeping me right about skateboards.

*He draws strength from the wingèd
cherubim and seraphim*

The lives

Vivaldi, the jumping cardinal, God and the number 3

Never having seen a sheep in Venice, junior-priest Antonio Vivaldi began counting cardinals instead, cardinals jumping off the papal balcony. Cardinal number one, then cardinal number two went leaping over the stone balustrade in a swirl of burgundy-and-scarlet cape.

It was one of those nights. No matter how hard he tried he just could not get to sleep. Lying on his left side, his right side, ten minutes flat on his back. Punch the pillow, then on to his left side again...His bedside clock showed the electronic red numbers flickering at 03:15. He willed them forward to 03:16. They refused to go.

He sighed, took a sip of water and lay down again. Too much wine with dinner? Not enough wine? The next cardinal paused before jumping, and spoke to him: 'The Holy Trinity is God's number and soon it will be yours, young Antonio.' He made the sign of the cross: 'God is giving you the number 3.'

'The number 3?'

'Yes, my son.' The voice faded as the burgundy-and-scarlet cape filled out and rose into the air. 'The number 3 will be yours.'

'Wait...! Wait...!' Vivaldi made a grab for the vanishing prelate. But God's emissary was already mere strands of coloured mist slipping through his fingers. Soon only a smell of incense remained, and he was alone once more.

'Shit! I'd actually been asleep!' Vivaldi gave the pillow an extra-hard thump, turned it over for coolness and lay back down again. But wearily, so very wearily. The number 3? In his imagination he could see the next batch of cardinals jostling to get in line at the rear of the balcony, like so many charter flights waiting for take-off. But he seemed unable to give them the all-clear. What was it with the number 3? Just then the church bell of San Giovanni chimed quarter past. Half past would be next. Then quarter to. Strike the hour, and they'd be back to quarter past again. Sleep was now further than ever.

Over the *caffè latte* and *panetto* next morning he remembered his strange dream, and had a good laugh. After a night like that he deserved a leisurely breakfast. He was late already, but so what? Becoming a junior-priest had never been his first choice – all that kneeling and standing, elevating the host and benedicting. His was a delicate constitution, a full-length mass often had him feeling pretty wrung out by the end, as well as a few kilos lighter from sweating under the holy vestments. But as the eldest son of a poor family – what were his options? He kept reminding himself it was better than working in McDonald's; and, at least, he wasn't expected to smile as he dished out the host and holy wine, or tell them to have a nice day.

Breakfast over, he stood up, brushed off the crumbs, donned the holy overalls, called goodbye to his mum and set off for San Giovanni's.

By the time he arrived, his twenty fellow-apprentices were standing in front of the altar, a chorus-line of swaying robes and bobbing hats, practising the day's routine. A priest was calling out, 'Father-Son-and-Holy-Ghost…Father-Son-and-Holy-Ghost…' Vivaldi slipped to the end of the line and, having caught the beat, joined in at making the sign of the cross.

Finally the priest clapped his hands for them to stop.

'Take five everybody. Our colleague, the recently arrived Signor Vivaldi, is going to give us a demonstration of how it should be done. He knows the moves so well he doesn't even need to get here on time to be shown them. So *he* can show us, the moves and the words *together*.' With a smile that was equal parts smugness and a sneer, he beckoned Vivaldi to the centre of the altar. 'If you please? I'll cue the "In-the-name-of-the..." and you'll take it from there. Let's say, twenty times? Just so we get the full benefit.'

Vivaldi took up position, facing the apprentices, who were arranged in a semicircle behind the priest: some were making faces, others sticking out their tongues. The priest glanced round to look at the boys and, immediately, as if some invisible force had preceded his gaze, their faces were smoothed back into looks of studious anticipation. When he turned to Vivaldi once more, the protruding tongues and rolling, bloodshot eyes were restored.

Vivaldi ignored them and began psyching himself up for performance. He stared into the middle distance, contemplating the emptiness of the pews beyond, the shafts of sunlight slanting down between the stone pillars, the shadows in the side-altars. Then something very unexpected happened.

He was well into his routine and gazing up at the decorated ceiling when, all at once, everything around him seemed to fade into the distance. He was still aware of the priest's voice calling, 'In-the-name-of-the...' and his own dutiful 'Father-Son-and-Holy-Ghost,' with his hands gesticulating in perfect time, when suddenly the church filled with an unearthly light. A light that was streaming directly at *him*!

Next came a flash of burgundy-and-scarlet, and *there* – hovering impossibly in mid-air, almost touching the ceiling with his holy hat – was his friend from the night before, the jumping cardinal.

'Greetings, Antonio!' Though the cardinal was manifesting himself a good thirty metres above, Vivaldi was aware of his voice as a whisper in his ear.

'God is speaking to you directly through me, but even He has His communication problems sometimes. If you can hear me, please nod.'

Vivaldi nodded.

'Good man!' The cardinal gave him the thumbs up. 'Now, you and I both know that all this dressing up, hand-waving and chanting is strictly for the birds: nothing but audio-visual aids, consumer-friendly signifiers of the Divine Presence. Agreed?'

Another nod from Vivaldi.

'Exactly. So, if you are ready, Antonio, God will now give you the number 3.'

'But I don't understand, I —'

The cardinal's hand was raised for silence. 'How you choose to use His gift is up to you. Most people are just given a life and left to get on with it — their loyalty points can be redeemed in heaven or hell. But *you* are different.'

Vivaldi looked blank.

'Let's be frank, Antonio. Priest-wise, you're never likely to amount to much, are you?'

Vivaldi shook his head.

'In fact, it's probably fair to say that the number 3 is all that stands between you and a career in hamburgers.'

Another nod from Vivaldi.

'So, how about telling the good Padre here that you suffer from asthma? The nodding and shaking you've been doing will look as if you've been gasping for breath. Tell him it's all too much for you. Tell him that, and you're out of here! *Capisci*?'

Another nod.

'Now, if you have ears to hear and eyes to see, God has something to show you.'

Already, the burgundy-and-scarlet cape was billowing to transparency, fold upon fold it was fading to nothing. A moment later it, and the jumping cardinal himself, were gone. Meanwhile, the stone arches that curved weightlessly, soaring upwards above the altar and pews to meet at the highest cross-point, seemed themselves to have shimmered into invisibility...into a series of chord progressions rising on all sides simultaneously to merge, layer upon layer, into a perfect harmony that held the unseen structure together.

Vivaldi fell to his knees. There was no stonework any more, no pews, no altar, no pillars, no walls, no windows, no church. Neither light nor darkness nor shadow. Only this perfect moment: utter concord, spreading out from one still point...Vivaldi closed his eyes, and God entered him as music.

He was carried home on a stretcher, and put to bed covered in poultices, leeches and an ice-pack. As a special treat his father brought through their new 24" – with black matrix screen and Fastext – and put the remote in his right hand, whispering words that would normally have thrilled: 'Today's an all-day Sergio Leone Special, back-to-back spaghetti westerns!'

Vivaldi managed to give his parents a smile as they left him, but less than five minutes into *A Fistful of Dollars* he had zapped it off. He wanted to relive that glorious epiphany in the church. He wanted to hear once more God's music within him.

He focused himself, he concentrated. And nothing happened. He forced himself to concentrate even harder. Still nothing happened. Silence. The harder he tried, the emptier and hollower the silence became. Eventually he slumped back exhausted. Exhausted, and bitterly disappointed. Heartbroken. Having heard God once, was he doomed never to hear Him again? Awash with suppurating poultices, leeches and melting ice, he lay on his bed and wept.

It was then that God received him. Vivaldi sensed Him as a strength and a tenderness beyond anything he had ever known. The Divine Presence began as rhythm. Not just as a rephrasing of the flow of time, mere skilful punctuation, but as a glimpse of eternity itself, patterned into purest form. An *allegro* of Divine Affirmation, expressed as a bass-line that thrummed to the very pulse of life. Then, as if from the Divine mouth itself, came the beginnings of a melody...

Vivaldi picked off a few leeches and reached for his quill.

Signora Vivaldi looked in to see how her son was. Fast asleep, the wee soul. Quietly she gathered up the mess of papers that had spilled off his bed on to the floor and put them tidily on his bedside table. Then she tip-toed out of the room, closing the door behind her.

His mother gone, Vivaldi peeked out from under his duvet. He glanced proudly over at the neat stack of music paper. His first concerto, for violin and strings. A symmetrical arch in three perfect movements, rising above and spanning the bustling abyss of everyday human clamour and chaos: *Allegro, Largo, Allegro*.

Time for a well-earned rest. Time for what remained of the Sergio Leone Special. If he was lucky he might still catch the closing scenes of *The Good, the Bad and the Ugly*. He reached for the remote, zapped straight to the film channel and snuggled back down with a sigh of contentment.

Seconds later, he was sitting up rubbing his eyes in disbelief: *A Fistful of Dollars*? It couldn't be...and the action wasn't much further on than before: near the beginning when the man with no name slouches his way up the main street towards the hired guns!

'Get some coffins ready,' he calls to the old undertaker.

Vivaldi stared at the screen: he'd been working nearly all day at the concerto, hadn't he? Well, hadn't he? Then, as though he were standing at the very threshold of the unknown, he paused. He felt himself in the presence of God and His mysterious ways. Was it possible that writing His music had taken – *no time at all*?

Just then the church bell of San Giovanni chimed quarter to, three strokes followed by silence. God had spoken. Vivaldi had heard and understood: no robes and funny hats for him, no holy hand-jive. God's message was loud and clear: 'I want three-movement concertos. Plenty of them and keep them coming!'

'So be it,' thought the ex-junior priest. He zapped off the TV and reached for his quill once more.

Vivaldi and the heavens' multicoloured luminous stars

No one could have been more surprised than Vivaldi when, turning up at the Aeroporto Marco Polo di Venezia, he was told that war had broken out. With all that single-minded attention to the brochures and the travel channel, he'd been completely unaware that country A had been threatening to liberate country B – or was it the other way round? Meanwhile, countries C and D had also become involved. It was then he noticed that everyone else in the terminal was carrying a machine gun, and what he'd taken for a courtesy bus parked outside the main door was actually a tank. He was the only passenger in sight.

'But – my holiday?' he asked the girl at the check-in desk.

She gave him a smile, and an apology for the lack of flights.

'But – I've written two hundred concertos,' he struggled to point out the urgency of his situation, 'and there are hundreds more to come. I need a break.'

The girl smiled again, and said nothing. She wore a name tag: *Lindy*.

'What will I do?'

'All holidays are cancelled, signor. It would be inappropriate while countries A, B, C and D are engaged in this struggle.

Inappropriate, sir – and your comfort and security could not be guaranteed.'

'But I'm booked to go to country E.'

'Same conditions apply.' She smiled again, 'My advice, signor, would be to go home and *pretend* you're on holiday. Get some multicoloured luminous stars from the gift shop, stick them on to your ceiling, climb into your sleeping bag and switch off the light. It will *seem* like country E, but even better: no dodgy water, dodgy food or dodgy plumbing.'

Only then did Vivaldi realise how much he had been looking forward to this break. He *longed* for it. The struggle to maintain diversity and invention in the limited form he had made his own had taken its toll, as had the constant return to first principles to ensure he remained close to the source of his own creativity. Under the weight of two hundred concertos, many of them for multiple instruments, he felt his life was all but crushed out of him. He stood in his holiday suit, holiday T-shirt and sandals, quite unable to think what to do next.

The check-in girl, meanwhile, had stuck a POSITION CLOSED sign on her counter. She unclipped her name tag.

'I've got to go now. Have a nice day.'

'You're leaving?' He stared at her. 'But what am I to do? Where am I to go?'

'You were the last one on the list. Now that you've turned up and your travel arrangements have been processed, my job is finished.'

To his surprise, Vivaldi heard himself ask: 'Lindy…? Would you like to come with me, to share the multicoloured luminous stars?'

'No.' She left.

Just then a man with a machine gun came up. 'You can't stay here, signor. There's a war on. Move.'

Vivaldi moved, wheeling his holiday suitcase behind him.

The taxi rank was empty. He trudged off down the road leading back to town. A convoy of tanks, armoured personnel carriers and missile transporters kept forcing him on to the verge and it wasn't long before he felt a stone in his shoe.

He stopped, took it out. Then carried on.

Ten minutes later, another stone. Another stop.

He carried on a little further. The sun shone. He was hot. He was thirsty. He was holidayless.

The first road block took him by surprise. Within seconds he was completely encircled by men with machine guns. One of them, a teenager with 'Private' on his name tag, stepped forward demanding, 'REFUGEE?'

'No, I'm from —'

'PASSPORT!'

After searching through a few pockets, Vivaldi handed it over.

The private passed it to an older, wearier-looking soldier who held it at arm's length before slowly bringing it closer to his eyes and into better focus. He was name-tagged 'Major', and was clearly drunk.

'Where did you get this passport?'

'It's mine. I'm from —'

'What's in the suitcase?' the major gestured that the private be given the key.

'My holiday stuff: spare T-shirts, spare sandals, shorts, socks and underwear; toiletries, pyjamas, sunglasses, suntan lotion, swimming trunks and a few concertos.'

The soldiers gathered round to look into the open suitcase. For several seconds no one spoke. A tank was waved through the road block.

The major swayed to and fro: an unsteadiness of grappa-breath, broken veins and exhaustion.

'Yes,' he grabbed on to a nearby private and hauled himself up straight, 'I've been in lots of war films. A stock character, really. The sensitive officer who's seen it all and no longer believes any of it. I go on about the futility of war, the waste of young lives. I drink to dull the pain.'

For a moment Vivaldi felt a surge of hope. 'This isn't a film, is it?'

'No, not any more.' The major took a bottle from his pocket, uncorked it and drank. 'So, you're a refugee?'

'No, I'm from —'

Just then the private whispered something in the major's ear, and both men looked away.

The major turned back almost immediately. He was holding a sheaf of music in manuscript: 'These concertos…?'

'Yes?' What if they didn't know anything about musical notation? What if they suspected it was a secret document, in code, and that he was a spy?

They addressed him, one after the other, with accusation in their eyes.

The major: 'There's nothing atonal here, is there?'
First private: 'The rhythmic patterns are consistent throughout all solo and ritonello passages?'
Second private: 'All modulations are well-argued, even those to distant and unrelated keys?'

'Yes…Yes…Yes.' He answered each man in turn, then fear made him start elaborating: 'No Second Viennese School for me. Occasional suspensions, of course, the odd accidental, but I can assure you that any dissonance is always within a tonal context.'

This reply was received with a round of the most beaming smiles. The major held up his bottle, courteously wiped the top with the palm of his hand, and offered it to him.

The grappa looked suspiciously cloudy and homemade. But he could hardly refuse…

Just then there was an explosion some thirty yards away and a small bed of zucchini vanished in a puff of smoke and green leaves. In response, the teenager-private pointed his machine gun at a clump of nearby trees and fired off a few dozen rounds.

'Don't you like grappa?' asked the major.

Vivaldi raised the bottle for the second time and pretended to take a deep swallow. He handed it back. In exchange, he received the key to his suitcase, which had been closed once more and presumably re-locked.

The major waved him through the barrier: 'Safe journey.'

All around, the bombardment was growing fiercer. The air was filled with drifting smoke, shells tore across the sky, mortars ripped into the fields, farmhouses and cottages on either side of the road; there were bursts of gunfire every few minutes. The military convoy now contained occasional lorry-loads of men and women crammed together, clutching cardboard boxes, plastic bags and children. No one spoke. As they drove by, they stared blankly at him wheeling his suitcase and dressed in his holiday best, rather dusty by this time from all the explosions. Whenever a tank rumbled past the ground shook.

Darkness was falling. The sleek staff cars, stretch limos with tinted windows, had their headlights full on.

Finally, a small red Nova pulled up beside him. At once, the vehicles behind started hooting, the drivers firing pistols and rifles into the air and shouting.

The window was wound down.

A woman's voice: 'Get in!'

Ten miles further on, having been driven entirely in second gear, the car shuddered to a halt.

'We're out of petrol,' Lindy, the check-in girl, leaned forward and pressed her face against the steering wheel. Behind her the convoy of lorries and missile transporters began hooting again. She ignored it.

'I've done everything I was ever asked to. Studied hard at school; sung in the church choir; only went out at weekends; kept clear of drugs, older men and gondoliers; passed my exams; got a job, my desk, my name tag. And for what? For *this*? To run out of petrol in the middle of nowhere, in the pitch dark, expecting to be blown to pieces at any moment?'

Vivaldi considered putting his hand on her shoulder, to comfort her. But was too shy.

'Do you have a spare can, maybe?'

'What the fuck do you think?'

He said nothing. They sat without speaking for several minutes.

Finally Lindy took out a tissue and dabbed her eyes. She blew her nose. 'We'll have to push it on to the verge. Come on.'

Having abandoned the car, they left the road and set off across open country. The moon was sliver-thin and, every few seconds, tracer bullets or exploding missiles and shells lit up the blackness, streaking it vivid red, orange and yellow. Then it was dark once more. In the distance they could hear the vehicles of military hardware and refugees trundling endlessly onwards.

He wanted to ask if this was a short cut back to Venice; he wanted to ask if his holiday tickets would be valid again in the near future. But he said nothing. He went stumbling across the ridges of a ploughed field...a particularly large explosion went off behind him...he turned and saw what might well have been their car going up in flames. His holiday suitcase, he now remembered, was still on the back seat. In all the panic he'd forgotten it. A holiday? What had he been thinking of? He pictured the quietness of his flat in the *sestiere,* near the Riva degli Schiavoni, and the calm pleasure, day after day, of adding to his steady output of concertos. Just then he saw a falling star; he closed his eyes and made a wish.

It was two hours before he knew for certain that his wish was never going to be granted. At first, the constant explosions had confused him – but now, as he scanned the night sky for the hundredth time, he was sure. Quite sure. And he was appalled.

'The stars. They're all in the same place.'

Lindy didn't even bother to glance up. 'Of course they are.'

'No – I mean, each one is in *exactly* the same place as it was earlier. They've not moved. It's like everything's come to a standstill. Except that now, some of them are *missing.*'

Over the next few minutes, several more constellations disappeared before their very eyes, as if they'd been chalk marks someone had casually wiped off the blackboard. Hundreds at a time. Vivaldi sensed the emptied darkness closing around them and felt Lindy's hand fumbling for his.

'What's happening...?' she whispered. The two of them stared up into the heavens. 'Are they shooting out the stars now?'

'Who knows *what* they are doing.'

Hardly more than fifty left. Just then, as if someone had gone round with a candle-snuffer, the stars of Canis Major and Canis Minor vanished one by one. Then Andromeda, Perseus and Cassiopeia. Less than thirty remained. Fifteen. Then ten. He put his arm around her as they watched until the last glimmerings of light had been extinguished.

If this had been the end of an opera, Vivaldi imagined to himself, the curtain would be pulled aside any second now, and the singers – the major and his soldiers, the tank commanders, lorry drivers, refugees, the entire cast, in fact – would each come forward into the glare of the stage lights to take a bow. There would be sudden applause, whistles and cries of *Bravo!*

But, instead, nothing happened. Absolutely nothing.

'Let's sit down,' said Lindy.

So they sat down.

And there, a few miles outside the city of Venice – with its world-famous canals, its glorious architecture, its historic churches – the two of them huddled together in the darkness, and began waiting.

Vivaldi learns a new skill

It's been only two weeks since Vivaldi learned to walk upon water, a real time saver in Venice. But for a man who normally writes a concerto faster than anyone can copy it, he's been slow to master this new skill. Despite living only a few streets away from the Pietà, the foundling home where he teaches the girls music and conducts the orchestra, he'd always been late for rehearsals. Finally, a seventeen-year-old with the voice of an angel and a distressingly pox-scarred complexion, took him aside. The girls rarely see men and then only through a screen of protective grille-work, so Vivaldi is often being taken aside – and his response never varies. He clutches his rosary even tighter and prays for deliverance.

Bianca had drawn him into a turret-style alcove off the Pietà's main hall, where the two of them were sealed into an intimacy of damp mist and the sounds and smells of the canal. She whispered: 'I'm not asking *why* you're always late, Maestro – but people are beginning to talk.'

'Talk?' repeated Vivaldi who had a particular fondness for the echo-effect in many of his multiple concertos.

'Gossip then. You're living with these two sisters and —'

'I've explained all that to the authorities. Many times. I'm not a well man, I'm an invalid near enough, and need —'

'These rehearsals, Maestro. They seem to get later and shorter every day – as it is, the girls can hardly keep pace with that three-movement conveyor belt you've got inside you.'

But Vivaldi had stopped listening. A distant foghorn sounding across the Rialto had given him an idea: 'Do you play the tuba?'

'Do I – what?'

'The tuba. I just thought: a concerto for tuba, mandolin and —'

'These rehearsals —'

'The sustaining brass sound-wall effect upon which the plucked strings —'

'These rehearsals, Maestro. It'll be much quicker by canal. Walking. I'll teach you.'

For once, Vivaldi stopped composing. He listened.

Ten minutes later he was standing at the top of a flight of steps leading down to the water's edge, standing and hesitating. Twice already he'd slipped on the mossy slime that clung to the stonework of this sunless backwater.

'You've got to be angry,' Bianca was saying. 'Really, really angry. Focus on that anger – on its precious energy – focus, then let it carry you forward.'

Vivaldi paused for a moment, uncertain whether to echo 'anger' or 'focus'. Then he shrugged.

'But what's there to be angry about?'

'You'll know, Maestro – just as I do. I focused all right. Pock marks like mine – my bad skin goes into a room first, and I follow after. I focused, I can tell you! Next thing I was halfway across the canal, and hardly getting my feet wet!'

Vivaldi was a kindly man: 'Poor child.' And he reached out to pat her. His right hand had let go of the rosary and for a split-second the young girl looked rather too much like a young girl. He grasped the rosary again, and held on.

'But what can I get angry at? I'm world-famous, five hundred concertos at the last count, nearly a hundred operas. My needs are taken care of by two sisters who —'

*The aerodynamically designed wellingtons
to reduce surface tension*

'Forget the sisters. I'll tell you something that'll get you really mad. Something about *you*.'

'Me? What about me?'

So she told him.

That was two weeks ago. Since then Vivaldi's never been late for rehearsals, not once, and is a familiar sight to gondoliers, walkers and loiterers on any bridge or canal side. If he has just hurtled past, there's usually a six-foot-high, ever-widening furrow of water behind him, and the buildings on either side echo his passing, as well they should. Only those Venetians alerted to his approach are fortunate enough to catch his cry of focused anger undistorted by the Doppler Effect, and make out what he is saying.

Indeed, here he is now, leaning over to take the corner into the Grand Canal without losing speed. See how the gondoliers notch their paddling up several gears to get out of the way, and even then they risk having their boats swamped.

Almost within range now. A lock of hair wisping out from under the wig, the macintosh frock coat, the violin in its spray-proof case, the aerodynamically designed wellingtons to reduce surface tension. Can you hear him?

'Bastard! Bastard! Stravinsky's a bastard!' And with that, he's blurred past already.

Why Stravinsky? you wonder. Why so much hatred for a man he's never met and never will meet? Bianca did well. Igor's opinion of Vivaldi's music really touched a nerve: 'Not five hundred concertos, but the same concerto five hundred times!'

Having focused once on that pithy little *bon mot*, Vivaldi's been jet-planing the canals of Venice ever since. Late at night he can be heard cruising up and down the fashionable stretches and calling out to whoever's at a jetty or leaning out their window, say, for one last look at this beautiful city before bed. He'll call to them: 'A neo-classicist! That's all Stravinsky is and all he'll ever be!'

Then he's swallowed up by the darkness. Behind him, water laps against the mossy stonework for a while, and then stills.

Alma Mahler leaves the nineteenth century behind

Alma Mahler lived in a series of glass boxes, one inside the other. Largest, and containing all the others, was the nineteenth-century-box, then Austria, then middle class, then woman, then home and so on…They were invisible. She could see people outside peering in, sometimes smiling, sometimes talking, sometimes waving hello. It must have been very tough glass because even when she hammered at it with both fists, the people continued smiling, talking and waving hello.

So there she was in the smallest of them all, at the very centre – the wife-box. She was always being told how pretty she was and how clever. Over the years she had come to pretend that, rather than being the one peering out, she was actually the one peering in – into the world all around her, at the swarms of fish-people mouthing bubbles of air.

That harmless deception got her through the days. The nights, however, were different. Very, very different.

One a.m., her husband fast asleep, Alma put on her warmest fur coat over her nightdress and crept silently downstairs to start work on her first string quartet. Having taken a few sheets of music paper from the bureau in his study, as well as pen and ink, she set herself down at the dining-table to work. Outside, the snow fell thickly on the cobbled streets till the wheel-ruts were erased and the city muffled to silence; inside, she scratched marks on the ruled paper, making it come alive with sound. Or, at least, that was the idea. Her string quartet refused to get beyond the few opening bars.

'Look,' she hissed at the hesitant second violin part, 'you're going to be in canonic imitation, and like it!' She finished the melodic phrase with an unexpected B flat for colour. Pleased with the start she'd made, she took a short break and went over to the window for a stare out at snow-white Vienna and its marzipan buildings with icing-sugar roofs. When she returned to her seat, she noticed the B flat had vanished. She peered closely at the rest of the second violin part. It too had vanished, completely. Not a note remained. And she was certain she'd written out the melody – quite certain.

'You bastard!' She wrote it out again. This time sustaining the B flat, just to be sure.

And that was when she noticed the opening notes of the first violin part growing faint. She sat and watched them disappear. Not only the sounds in the street but those in her head, too, were being overlaid with the silence of falling snow. The perfectly conceived opening section – which had forced her out of bed in the first place – had now completely vanished, as if it had never been.

'Bugger!' She wrote it out for the third time, making her way down the quartet stave: 'That's your part, first violin…and yours, second…and yours, viola…and yours, cello.' As a test she wrote *Hello Alma!* on a piece of scrap paper. Time for a cup of coffee.

Coffee break over, she returned from the kitchen and picked up the message she'd written to herself. Yes, both words were still there. Then she glanced at the quartet.

Not one single note remained.

She'd have to start all over again. New pen, fresh music paper. Quickly, quickly. This time the ideas seemed to fly from her pen

*'You bastard!' She wrote it out again. This time sustaining the
B flat, just to be sure*

faster than she could write and, once on the paper, they seemed to stay there. At last, she was getting somewhere. Handel had a reputation for being able to compose a six-part fugue faster than anyone could write a letter. Well, she laughed to herself, here was *Frau* Handel!

Having finished the introduction and the first few bars of an *allegro,* she paused. Took a sip of cold coffee. Alma Mahler's String Quartet Number One – this was the stuff to give them! No more middle-class civilities and amateurism, but real commissions and hard cash.

She was tired but determined to keep going.

Finally, after getting to her feet for another glance out of the window, she sat down again…and was just in time to see the last notes she'd written disappear.

That night she dreamed she was a singing fish. The most wonderful music seemed to fill her, making her every movement a thing of grace and beauty: but with not a sound to show for it.

The following afternoon she decided to tell her husband.

And here he was, striding up the path: Gustav Mahler, composer, opera director and man of genius. She was always amazed at the ease with which he passed through his boxes. He was peering at her now. She peered back, smiling. Their lips touching the layer of glass between them in a kiss. He began talking, waving his arms like only a successful conductor could and pausing every few minutes for her to nod or shake her head in reply. Finally, he gave her the look which told her it was her turn.

She brought out the music manuscript and was showing him the inexplicable blank staves when the maid came in with *kaffee und Sachertorte.* The young girl spread a neat linen cloth, then laid out the cups and saucers, the plates, the napkins. Alma noticed that the girl's feet didn't seem to touch the floor and, on leaving, she glided out on an unseen current, through the doorway and into the hall.

Gustav had begun talking again. Alma was too distracted to make out the words — not that they really mattered. She recognised his 'explaining' face, as she called it. Her husband was explaining something to her; his mouth opened and closed, words came out and, in this way, problems were dealt with. Her manuscript of invisible music was being shown to her, lifted from the table, put down again, lifted up again. Gustav was smiling now. Clearly, the problem had been addressed and dispatched. His 'reassuring' face was telling her not to worry. *Kaffee und Sachertorte* finished, he rose from the chair, gave his body a flick and glided effortlessly out of the room, just like the maid had done.

His movement, followed by the opening and closing of the door, created a series of after-ripples that set the carpet, the curtains and the walls swaying. Even the marble firmness of the clock-face shuddered.

Alone, Alma swam back and forth in her box, her tail thrashing, her head hitting against hard glass at every turn. Outside she could see twilight beginning and the lamplighter making his rounds. Soon it would be dark. From the study next door came the sound of her husband playing his piano. No matter how much she twisted and turned, she felt the vibrations resonate through the entire length of her body, like blows.

That night, clad once more in her fur coat and nightdress, Alma emerged from her fish-dream and went downstairs. The house was completely silent. The heavy carpets absorbed her footfalls, the heavy hangings silenced her passage, deadening every sound. She was a ghost in her own home.

Only when she'd closed the door behind her did she dare light the lamp. She placed the glass globe over the wick and, at once, a soft light spilled across the study. The stolidity of the cumbersome daytime furniture was now turned into half-shadow, varnish-sheen and crystal.

The piano stood in the corner, a walnut-brown Bechstein baby-grand, a curve of pure weightlessness. She crossed the floor and sat down. A pile of music lay on top, Gustav's neat hand-written notations for *Das Lied von der Erde* covering page after page.

A sudden irrational thought: when she touched these keys, there would be no sound. Nonsense, of course. But the notes of her string quartet had been disappearing…Was she going mad? No. Not yet anyway, she laughed to herself. Then she lifted the lid.

One afternoon years later, while posing for her lover, the painter Oskar Kokoshka, she remembers that night in wintry Vienna when she'd sat down at her husband's piano and played one note, then another and another. Gradually, her hesitancy had given way to confidence, and her confidence to total abandon. Soon she'd been battering at the keys, full-force. Loud, and ever louder. When she stopped, the echo resonated around the study walls and ceiling. A glance at the clock: she'd been playing for nearly a quarter of an hour. Hadn't Gustav heard? Or the maid? Her children? No one had come to see what was happening, to applaud, to protest even. There she'd sat, in her fur coat and nightdress, like some madwoman. In the silent untroubled house.

'Don't shut your eyes.'

Almost dozing off, is she? Kokoshka's head bobs back out of sight behind the canvas. A moment later it's out again looking at her. In and out, in and out. Now you see me, now you don't.

Finally, just as first light was showing outside, she'd closed the piano lid, turned down the lamp and left the room to go upstairs. Pausing in the hall, she could almost feel the emptiness of the streets all around the house. The terrible silence. Like a city drowned. Like herself.

She'd climbed the stairs to their bedroom, every step had creaked, and every movement was a sigh. She paused every so often to let the silence catch up.

'Alma, don't shut your eyes.'

Kokoshka's voice brings her back from the past, returning her to the sunlit studio with its slanted glass roof. In the corner a tap drips into a paint-spattered sink. She's been listening to its steady *drip...drip...drip* nailing her to complete immobility for the last half-hour. She keeps her eyes wide open. There are no glass boxes any more, no wife-box, no Vienna-box, no nineteenth century. That night, as she'd made her way up to their room, everything around her had started giving way, cracking apart. She'd reached the head of the stairs and paused, utterly unprotected.

Ever since then she's been walking on broken glass.

'Don't shut your eyes, I said.' *Drip...drip...drip...* Now you see me, now you don't...

Then she hears her lover say that today's sitting is finished. Without turning her head, she glances up towards the slanted roof. Outside, it is a lovely summer's day. She can hear motor engines, the rumble of metal wheels, a tramcar; from far in the distance come the cries of what might be someone shouting, singing or maybe even screaming.

Time to relax, time to ease herself from the afternoon's pose. She stretches forward to place her foot on the ground, to let it take her weight. Bracing herself for the lacerating pain she knows will come.

How Bach won the battle against modern technology

The parcel was half a metre high, cube-shaped and wrapped in shiny red paper. It stood next to his breakfast plate: tied with large wreaths of gold tassel and addressed in a scrolled script of suitably baroque loops and curves.

'Not another one!' said Bach, shoving it aside and reaching for the marmalade. Down the Initials' end of the table young CPE, JC and WF were squabbling about the future of Late Baroque, throwing crusts at each other to settle whether the advent of digital technology would elevate contrapuntal writing to ever-greater heights or render it obsolete. CPE was accused of clinging to outmoded harmonic practices; JC's Early Classicism would lead only to base salon music, came the spirited reply. WF looked on gravely and said nothing. He was the eldest of Bach's Initials and, all his brief life, had been subjected to the full weight of parental expectation. Even at such an early age, he knew sorrow.

Breakfast over, Bach turned to his unopened parcel and sighed. He could guess what it contained. Kapellmeisters, however, were expected to be grateful. After the first half-dozen similar such gifts, he had run off fifty form letters of grovelling thanks appropriate to his humble station. In the circumstances, none of the recipients would want a mere handwritten effort. Deference was easy, the real problem was what to do with the damn things. Ever since that article, 'If Only Bach Had A Computer', appeared in the previous month's *Digital Digest*, the house had been filling up. Anna Magdalena, as she made increasingly clear after each special delivery, was getting more than a little annoyed at the loss of storage space. Her linen cupboards were bulging with monitors, printers and keyboards; there were laptops stacked on the stairs and windowsills; the bath brimmed with new software packages; whenever a door opened or closed, white polystyrene filler drifted across the floor like miniature tumbleweed. Disks were being used as coasters, fibre-optic cable doubled as clothes-lines and, more importantly of course, as goal-netting.

Forget the high-tech information revolution, Bach said to himself and got to his feet, he still had his Goldberg Variations to finish, twenty-three down and seven more to go. 'Something to cure me of my insomnia' had been the ambiguously worded commission from Count Keyserlingk: 'My man can play it to me during the long sleepless hours.' Poor 'my man' Goldberg, woken at 3 a.m. to play the same aria and thirty variations over and over until his Countship felt ready to drift off. Thought JSB to himself: that's one harpsichord player who'll be dropping me from his Christmas card list.

But first, the form letter. *Most Gracious ——, In deepest humility I wish to offer my profoundest gratitude for your bounteous gift of an Apple/Sony/Compaq/Amstrad/other which I will find of inestimable* (that, at least, is true) *aid to me in my work* (blah, blah). *You cannot understand what it will mean to me* (also true) *and I will endeavour* ...(blah, blah, blah).

Could he put his name to such a document?

Yes, he'd done it before and, God willing, would do it again. He bent down to embark upon his signature, a pen-flourish so dizzyingly and psycho-pathologically intricate that he had to look up afterwards towards the horizon, to steady himself. And as he did so, he caught sight of the Initials out in the yard playing football.

Goldberg could wait. JSB clambered on to a nearby Apple monitor to get a better view through the leaded glass. When a young man, he too had wanted to play the beautiful game. Indeed, he had once made the two-hundred-kilometre journey to see Dietrich Buxtehude, who was on long-term contract to Lubeck. At sixty-eight years of age, the grand old man was a living legend. Unfortunately, Bach tried hitchhiking his way there, dressed only in his Arnstadt strip and shorts. A bad move. Not a single lift – he ended up walking the whole two hundred kilometres, and arrived too late. By the time he limped into the town the tabloids were screaming DIETER QUITS! and BUXTEHUDE IN BOOTS-OFF SHOCKER! It seemed that the maestro had kicked his last ball and, overnight, withdrawn from the game. He'd opted for a sedentary retirement: his football skills devoted to the bass-pedalling of the cathedral organ while the rest of him pulled out stops and pushed down keys.

Undaunted, young Bach turned up day after day in the hope of getting a game started. If only his idol would come down from the draughty organ loft and get back on to the pitch where he belonged! Over the next two months, Johann almost froze to death standing on the stone floor in his shorts and stocking soles (he'd been told to leave his muddy boots at the cathedral door). At last Buxtehude acknowledged him. And a sorry sight the young hopeful had become: the now-sagging ball, the unrolled stockings, the solitary shin-pad, and the sense of a trust betrayed that, sooner or later, finds expression on a child's face turned too long towards the adult world. Then the idol spoke.

Sadly, by the time Bach had staggered out into the sun and once more warmed himself back up to body temperature, he'd forgotten his master's exact words. But their import was clear, and the lesson learned.

Within minutes, he'd ditched the shorts, swapped the boots for a wig and matching trousers, and got a lift back to Arnstadt first flick of the thumb.

'Organist, are you?' asked the lorry driver, appraising him cool as you please.

Pausing only for dramatic effect, Bach kept his gaze fixed on the road straight ahead and announced: 'Organist, improviser *and* composer!'

Bach was never to kick a ball again. Now, as he watched the Initials playing three-and-in he smiled to himself, then rapped on the window-pane and shouted at them to get on with their morning scales. Still smiling as he climbed off the monitor, he couldn't resist giving it a heartfelt big toe to nowhere. He was pleased to see the AppleMac bounce several times across the tiles: he knew that not all computers bounced so well. He had tried them.

Over the years Bach mellowed, digitalwise. He grew older, he surfed and, from time to time, he downloaded.

One day, just as he was working towards the climax of his monumental *Art of Fugue* – he'd reached a particularly tricky point in the concluding triple fugue shortly after the exposition of the third subject – his computer crashed. He stared at the screen, at the notes frozen into position on the staves and the empty space that would now never be filled. Luckily, he had installed a new software programme that saved all new data instantly. But it would still mean disconnecting this and disconnecting that, it would mean lugging the thing round to the engineer, it would mean recovering the hard disk, it would mean...

Enough was surely enough. With one deliberate and satisfying tug he pulled the plug clear from the wall.

At peace now, he sat enjoying a moment of post-electronic wistfulness. As if on cue, from through the open window came the liquid melody of a blackbird's song. He sighed to himself and whispered as if in reply: 'No more fugues, no more fugues...'

Beethoven's response to the hanging gardens of neglect

'BECOME A MILLIONAIRE IN SIX MONTHS — OR EVEN LESS!' had been the 20-point, bold-type heading to the flyer that had come in the second post. Beethoven studied it carefully. There was no small print, just promises, testimonies from newly minted millionaires, multicoloured graphs and persuasive statistics. Knowing where his best interests lay, the great composer had put aside the sketches of a new symphony.

That was yesterday. Today, as always, he's come striding into Edinburgh. Setting a cracking pace up Minto Street — a gradient that defeats many a lesser musician — picking up speed on the flat so that 8 Till Late, Bernie the Barber's single-room single-chair salon, Blockbusters, the Queen's Hall and South Clerk Street itself are no more than a blur of shop windows and stalled traffic. Steamrollering down Nicolson Street, hitting peak form opposite Tesco. Looking neither right nor left — no glance into the Apple Centre nor towards Chandler's Classical Music shop (vinyl a speciality). No distractions — he's utterly focused. The other pedestrians part to let him through, the buildings on either side seeming to lean back to give him freer passage: the iron railings of

Nicolson Square, the glass-walled Festival Theatre, the soot-blackened Old Quad. Neither too fast nor too slow, *allegro ma non troppo*, the colossus of western music marches ever onwards.

Knowing he's going to be a rich man has certainly put a spring in Beethoven's step this morning – and no wonder! By 3 p.m. yesterday every scrap of available paper had been covered in calculations – and he knew he couldn't lose. By 4 p.m. he'd been to the bank, withdrawn £2,000 in ten-pound notes. Called at the post office on his way home. By 6 p.m. he'd been writing letters. By midnight addressing envelopes. By 2 a.m. licking stamps. Three in the morning had seen him and a sackful of mail staggering towards the nearest post box.

The future's looking good. There'll be no more selling the same old *Mass in C* over and over to different publishers pretending it's brand new, no more depending on handouts, sponsorship deals and brown-nose dedications. Strictly business class from now on: stretch limos and platinum cards. He'll be a frequent flyer, hitting the executive hospitality suite to make up for all those years trapped in the bus lane of life.

As the rest of us get into the swing of the new millennium, we seem to have lost touch with the basso continuo keeping us in step with our individual destinies. No primal rhythm moves us any more, only a debased counterpoint of hopes and fears, regrets and self-interest. We have stumbled, and have been brought to our knees. Not so Beethoven.

Brushing aside the rise and fall of several empires, the discovery of the subconscious, the splitting of the atom and a world war upon which the sun has never quite set – the great composer sticks to his chosen path. When it rains, he gets drenched to a perfect likeness of the portrait done shortly after his first set of cello sonatas: black hair, a sleekness and confidence of demeanour, a youthful moisture about the cheeks, lips and eyes. When sleet sharpened by an easterly comes scudding in off the Forth, he ages to that grey-haired Bürgermeister of the late quartets: the straggled locks, the complexion of liver rolled in flour. But whatever the weather, he never lets his gaze shift from the far horizon as if only from *there* – Portobello Beach? The shimmering hills of Fife? – will come any hope for the salvation of mankind. But who knows? Perhaps it will.

Now that he's passed the Chinese Buffet King, one of the city's major landmarks looms into view, the Tron Kirk – as tantalising as ever. Only a few hundred metres to go, but Beethoven has never yet succeeded in reaching its ever-beckoning steeple. Before him lies the most difficult part of his journey – the Zone of Everything-and-Nothingness that is South Bridge. The great composer has never yet conquered this no man's land, this anti-matter force-field, between Infirmary Street and the Royal Mile...And already he's slowing down, stumbling even. Beneath these pavements are the layers upon layers of darkness, the walled-up passages and hidden chambers whose forgotten stonework long ago became the foundations for today's Festival City. Like some terrible gravity, the city's stifled history has begun dragging on his every step.

He struggles to keep going, pausing every few yards to catch his breath. Soon he's hauling himself hand-over-hand from doorway to lamp-post to bus shelter, to have something always to hold on to. Finally, next to Poundstretcher's, he stops, and doesn't get started again. He can go no further. Here, indeed, is a stretch of Dante's dark wood: perpetually failing daylight, the fast food outlets one after the other, the roomfuls of slot machines, the suitcase sellers, the hirers and lenders and cheque cashers, the MASSIVE SALES where the whole world itself will be marked down in the end. The message is clear: EVERYTHING MUST GO. This is the twenty-first century – overlaid by swirling litter, scaffolding and dogshit.

Seeking relief, Beethoven lifts his eyes to above street-level, and sees floor upon floor of boarded-up windows, peeling paintwork, untenanted dampness, mould and dry rot. Upwardly mobile decay that's held in check by the weight of chimney-stacks and roof-lead, by the rattle of broken slates, the snap and slash of exposed wiring and, most of all, by the hanging gardens of neglect: the wind-borne grass and weeds clinging to choked gutters and shattered stonework.

With both hands raised, the great man has stepped off the pavement and out into the middle of the street.

'ENOUGH!'

His anguished cry reverberates along the entire length of South Bridge. The traffic comes to an abrupt halt. He climbs into the nearest taxi.

'TREES!' he commands. 'Take me to trees, and meadows. And rushing streams. And hills.'

Meter switched on, the driver glances in the mirror to inspect his latest fare.

His latest fare stares straight back at him: 'Trees, I said. Big ones. Big branches, broad leaves, trunks like gasometers.'

'Certainly, sir. Trees it is. The Botanics maybe?'

'The trees of my Sixth Symphony, the *Pastorale* in F major Op.68, did not grow in the Botanics! They were not watered by council hoses nor clipped by council shears. I want wild trees, not ones with labels on them! I want trees of freedom reaching for the heavens! I want wide open spaces and a horizon that expands the soul!'

'Fair enough, sir.' The driver does a quick u-ey, turning his taxi to face the way he'd just come.

Maxi-the-taxi is used to tourists. His childhood among religious fanatics has secured him an equable temper based on the certain knowledge of his own salvation. It cheers him to think that he himself brings thousands of city-visitors that bit closer to their predestined damnation – and gets paid for it. His psychopathology is strictly Scottish throwback. Like most children, he was musical. In the absence of an orchestra in his muddy village he conducted the hedges and woodlands, his string section. As he grew more confident, the sheep and cattle on the hillside, the clouds, the birds, the wind, the river, the farmer's dog, his tractor – everything seen and unseen was given its place on his unwritten score. So far so good – then word got around. His teacher, a strict believer in Scottish education, stood him out in front to conduct the morning's noise, and kept him there till he'd learned his lesson. That night young Maxi lay in bed listening to the restless hills and streams, to their unplayed music. Far above him, the moon turned soundlessly on its invisible rope.

Adult Maxi nourishes the child-within by picturing the torments his passengers are destined for. It passes his days. As they reach Minto Street, towards the unmapped Southside lying beyond Cameron Toll and out of town, he switches to automatic pilot and starts revelling in visions of damnation. A faith-strengthening exercise.

For Beethoven looking out of the taxi window, the journey's like watching his recent past unscroll backwards before his very eyes: the Festival Theatre, the Apple Centre, Queen's Hall, Blockbusters, Bernie's. For consolation, he reminds himself that two hundred letters (minimum required) with a ten-pound note (no cheques, please) in each, are even now making their way to the potential contributors to his future wealth. The hard work has been done, all that remains is to let the Karmic tide of fiscal benevolence roll back in, swamping him with cash.

'The Pentlands suit you then, sir?' Maxi's called from the front of the cab.

The great composer is savouring his calculations one more time. Even allowing for a modest response rate, 10% say, he'll get a tenner from 20 of them – 20×10. £200. Plus a further tenner from each of the replies they themselves receive in turn – 20×20×10. £4,000. Then tenners from everyone that replies to all of *them*. Which'll be the same again, times ten. £40,000. And so on, and so on, and so on...The mind boggles.

'THE PENTLANDS, SIR? Are you deaf?'

'No need to shout.'

Twenty minutes later the taxi has pulled up at the Flotterstone road-end.

Beethoven stares out at the grass-and-bracken slopes of Turnhouse

Hill and Carnethy, at the green fields and generous stretches of woodland. There is an ache in his heart and a longing too deep for words. Which would he like to do first: lay his head on Nature's grassy bosom, or hug a few trees?

'That'll be £22.40.'

Beethoven takes out his purse. 'Do you take *groschen*?'

'£22.40.'

'Euros?'

'£22.40.'

'Cheque? Switch? Mastercard? Tele-transfer?'

Maxi is a super-bigot in financial matters also. Though more enlightened Calvinists accept the elegance of double-entry book-keeping and the dynamics of credit as God's gifts to the prudent, Maxi considers such innovations to be 'limbs of Satan'. Since the economic boom of the '80s, he has watched Satan's limbs multiply exponentially and it is one of his bitterest pleasures to hunt down and damn every new ISA, TOISA and MIRA.

Too late Beethoven hears the twin *clicks* of the taxi doors' automatic locks.

It is evening. After a cup of sweetened tea and a dinner of bread followed by bread, Beethoven prepares to stretch out on his Scottish Office regulation strip of bed-foam. Having been driven, at no extra charge, to St Leonard's police station, he has decided that, this time, he really has *had* it. From further down the corridor come the sounds of a man weeping, another is screaming. In the cell next door someone's hammering his fists against the wall: 'Sticking me back in here again! See you, God, you've a fucking short memory!'

Beethoven switches off his hearing aid. Peace at last, time out from the headlong rush of human progress and the miracle that is pyramid-selling. Like the descending violin figure from the Benedictus of his *Missa solemnis*, he gradually eases himself into a state of complete calm. This moment of delicious resignation, he considers, should not be squandered on the contemplation of mortality nor on thoughts of a new string quartet. It is precious, and should be treasured. He lies back and closes his eyes...

Maxi, meanwhile, is nearing the end of his backshift. He's begun talking to himself: 'Got hissel immortality wi symphonies? – but he disnae pey his wey. Only yin place fer the likes of thon. Stick him in, an throw away the key.'

Nobody listens, of course. His last fare is a woman giving birth. As he drives away from the hospital Maxi consoles himself for the lack of a tip: 'Anither yin tae keep the fires burnin.'

Thanks to some joint funding from the Scottish Arts Council and the Goethe Institute, Beethoven is released a few days later.

Naturally, he wants to hurry straight home to the pile of accumulated mail – every envelope swollen with hard cash. But he doesn't. Because he can't. Because he is utterly lost. Decanted after midnight on to an unfamiliar street, without map or directions. Where is his customary route? The shops he knows so well? The theatres, galleries, restaurants?

He wanders a city of darkened streets. All around him are the eyes that glare, the tongues that loll, the hands that clench and claw, the faces turned inside-out. He blunders from pavement to gutter and back on to pavement again, slithering on vomit, piss and pizza. He gets shouted at, sworn at. He's grabbed, punched, kicked. There are only the hard men left – the hard men, and the downtrodden. All of them had been set free in *Fidelio*, only to be imprisoned once more, it seems, here in the free market. In this nightmare, all he can summon to his aid – like a set of bearings for another place, another time – is the enigmatic phrase he scribbled in the margin of his last string quartet.

Coming to an abrupt halt at a traffic island in the middle of nowhere, he glowers in every direction, then raises a clenched fist to the heavens. He cries out: 'MUST IT BE? IT MUST BE!'

Each curse he brings down upon the city is marked ff.

Johannes Brahms goes in search of his first symphony

For the last few months the city of Hamburg had come to a complete standstill; the hands of every clock and watch remained stuck at a quarter to five on a winter's evening. The sea mist that had once soaked into the cobbles and saturated the masonry of the houses now oozed back out of the stonework like so much chilled sweat; the rigging of the motionless ships on the Elbe hung slack with moisture that dripped and dripped…Low sagging cloud and the Baltic seeped into each other along a horizon that was never more than a few yards away.

Everyone knew it was Brahms's fault. For twenty years the composer had been unable to complete his first symphony. Into the drawer, out of the drawer, too good to bin, not good enough to perform…and all the while frittering away his creativity in string serenades and clottedly scored chamber music. Finally, the sheer weight of his symphonic inertia had brought all daily life around him to a halt. To his fellow-citizens it seemed this blighted November evening had been going on for ever. They aged, and had nothing to show for it. Eternity of a sort.

Brahms got up from the overstuffed sofa where he'd been working hard, scratching out every last one of the notes he'd scratched in the previous day. The sheets of music paper fell to the floor; he kicked them across the room and felt better. Then felt worse. He crossed to the window, wiped the clouded glass and looked out. Everything was exactly the same as last time: a twilit gloom turning into early darkness and, set in the windows opposite, candles perpetually on the point of guttering out.

Somewhere above there was a sky, but would he ever see it again? He rubbed at the glass once more. At the best of times 4:45 p.m. is a low point of any day, but this unbroken run had taken its toll: the oil portraits were flaking, there was a brittleness to the furniture, the parquet-flooring creaked with uncertainty, on his mantelpiece the porcelain shepherdesses were exhausted from holding the same momentary pose without release.

His own fault, of course. If only he hadn't insisted on making such a big fuss about Beethoven.

Brahms stared out at the accumulated misery. With life on hold, it was a relief to get back to picking at the same old scab – Beethoven. If the great man hadn't completed his symphonic output with that final, no-holds-barred, choral movement, then maybe Brahms's generation might have had a chance to...

The composer gave himself a thump on the side of the head that set his ears ringing: he must stop whingeing. So Ludwig Van had said it all. Big deal. Time to move on.

'My first symphony!' he announced to the portraits, then marched himself across the room. 'It's out there somewhere, and I'm going to find it.' He banged the door behind him to encourage himself down the stairs and out into the street.

'He's young,' excused the portrait of Haydn.

'Not *so* young,' pointed out an also-ran of the Mannheim School whose eyes had recently begun to show the hurt of disappointment lying just under the oil paint, varnish and neglect.

There seemed nothing more to be said, so the portraits fell silent. Three left-overs from the *Sturm und Drang* movement threw a collective moody and turned their faces to the wall.

*

Outdoors, nothing had changed. The strain of perpetual twilight was beginning to tell: stone cellars were turning to moss and lichen, plants were wilting, tiled stoves in danger of cracking with the build-up of unexpended heat. Everywhere Brahms went, stolid burghers of the city glared after him.

He came to the harbour, and here a surprise awaited him. Normally grim and purposeful, the landlocked seafarers had taken the opportunity of this enforced slack period to call in a fashionable designer. The result was a multi-choice seafront-makeover that reminded the composer of those clever, magic-eye postcards he had seen on his recent holiday to Tenerife, showing different views according to how the picture was tilted. In the right hand corner of this state-of-the-art cyber-harbour there was a menu. Why settle for a dour Hanseatic port? He need only click the cursor to call up a yachting marina in the Bahamas, a Fife sea-wall, the reclaimed coastal strip in Manama City, Bahrain. Brahms knew an invitation to lethargy when he saw it, and made his choice.

He stepped carefully across the empty beach, not wanting to disturb the angle-of-tilt which would cause the palm trees and little oil pumps raising and lowering their heads into the sand like so many young ostriches, to dissolve around him. Trapped for ever in the instant of its creation, the tide on the Bahrain coast surged forward, only to be drawn back with a relentless hiss of frustration.

For most of his life Brahms had known only the worn-out grey fading to threadbare dinginess of northern gloom, but here was brightness and light! Here the sky was paint-box blue, ditto the sea, the sand was buttercup-yellow relieved by occasional scribbles of shiny black to illustrate rocks. This stretch of coast had been reclaimed from the ocean floor; it was a completely new world. Where else but here would he find a completely new symphony?

The composer was happy. The scene looked so fresh and newly painted that he actually joked to himself: if he touched anything, might he not leave smudge marks? Were he to amble over to the right-hand corner, might he not find a signature? Brahms rarely joked and certainly *never* ambled. After a few hesitant steps he paused. Took his bearings. Eased himself a few degrees further from true and took a few more steps. This, he assured himself, was ambling.

The sea, as anyone who lives near it well knows, is a living thing. It is the largest living thing on the planet. A manic-depressive with severe mood swings, it is both playful and predatory. Thanks to its pounding and grabbing, what started out long ago as one continent is now several, and the sea has them all surrounded. In time, the melting ice-caps will do the rest...

The sea watched Brahms as he ambled. The composer was concentrating so exclusively on being Mr Carefree Ambling Stroller that he didn't notice the occasional wave edging nearer. For once in his life he'd stopped worrying about following in Beethoven's footsteps. Indeed, he'd just joked to himself that here, at least, were no footsteps at all save his own – when he suddenly noticed his feet were wet. So much for ambling, he thought. But these were not the Baltic waters with their bone-clutching iciness, these waters were deliciously warm. There was no one to see him: and so, off with the shoes and socks, roll up the trouser legs and there he was – paddling! He laughed out loud, he was really, really happy.

The sea purred around him, salting his flesh...

For the first time in years Brahms felt lighter; the water was now lapping up to his Teutonic knees, supporting him; it bore the weight of his disappointment, it relieved him of his anxieties.

He began ambling all over again. He frolicked. He cavorted. He splashed. But his anxieties and self-doubts about following after Beethoven had become so much part of him that, as the sea absorbed them, it began absorbing *him* too.

His reflection was first to go. He gazed in disbelief as the colours making up his image grew indistinct, then gradually grew more transparent. Briefly the water around him became cloudy. And all at once, it cleared.

His reflection was no longer there.

Like a candle melting into a vast pool of wax, the rest of him quickly followed.

Soon all that remained were a few floating bristles and a certain undischarged tension. Then that, too, faded to stillness. Had anyone else been there, they would have heard the sea sigh with contentment.

Back in Hamburg, with the finger of Brahms's stalled creativity no longer pressing on the Pause button, Time began moving slowly forward. The November evening got itself back up to speed. 4:45 became 4:46 became 4:47. In due course, the moon rose, streetlights came on, trains resumed their accustomed timetables, dinners were cooked and eaten, children were loved and scolded and sent to bed. The great composer was not missed.

The following night it rained – and how! A ferocious heavens-emptying deluge that was more organ-pipes than stair-rods. It battered the roof tiles and windows, it set rones brimming and gushing, it swelled gutters to overflowing, flooded drains, sluiced down streets and left them awash. Having been evaporated up into the atmosphere, Brahms, as it were, now descended upon the city. The noise he made when coming down as rain anticipated the orchestral effects that came to be known as the Johannes Brahms Sound: the thickened texture of strings and woodwind, the thumping timpani and that rasp of distant brass as the wind changed direction.

Morning dawned clear and cloudless. Brahms had been dispersed widely across the city from downtown Reeperbahn to the suburbs of Blankenese. Scattered here, there and everywhere, he was gathered in pools, puddles, waterbutts and drains. Like the beginnings of life on earth, the composer's scattered molecules were a DNA accident waiting to happen. All that was needed was a miracle.

*

Brigitta was fourteen years old and very proud of her long blonde hair. But braided or brushed free? That was always the big question. After the distress of the previous night's storm she had decided that today was a brushed-free day, though already she was having second thoughts. Her would-be boyfriend, Jürgen, trailed after her as she walked through town. He was hopelessly smitten and did everything a young man could do to secure her attention: he shouted her name, he whistled, he threw crisp packets and sticky sweets at her. Dodging these cupid-darts she skipped lightly from shop window to shop window as if going from stepping stone to stepping stone across the pleasurable day.

Unable to sleep for the noise of the rain, Jürgen had spent most of the night reading the latest page-turner from Hans Christian Anderson, and thinking about Brigitta. Now, seeing her pause to gaze questioningly at her reflection in a milliner's window, he was taken by a glorious inspiration: 'My mermaid! My mermaid!' he called out.

Brigitta flushed with embarrassment, and pleasure. She permitted him a smile, then ran off up the street jumping flirtatiously over puddles and gutters. Two streets away was her secret place, a house belonging to a rich Hanseatic merchant who seemed always away on his Hanseatic travels. Since the beginning of the year his garden had been left to go to rack and ruin. Neglected, it had flourished. Glancing behind her now to check that Jürgen was not in sight, she slipped through the side gate and into the overgrown garden.

Moments later she was kneeling by the small pool that was the most secret place of all — a tangle of waterlilies, weeds and stillness. She smoothed the surface with her hand to clear away the reflected clouds and overhanging branches. A mermaid, she repeated to herself. A beautiful young mermaid. She drew her long blonde hair through her fingers. Her skin was glowing, pulsing with unfamiliar longings and hormones. Finally she leaned over the water...

A kiss to greet her reflection, or to bid it farewell for ever? There was an intimacy to the moment that she had never known before. And a seriousness. The water tasted salty. As she stood up, she couldn't help but wipe her lips with the side of her hand. When she walked away, she carried herself with a new dignity and purpose. She left the merchant's neglected garden, and never returned.

Once begun, the chain reaction set up by the touch of Brigitta's lips on her own reflection moved with exponential acceleration. A couple of hours later, Johannes Brahms, the molecularly reconstituted composer, rose from the clouded surface of the pool and stepped on to solid ground once more. He looked around the unfamiliar garden and couldn't even summon up a gasp of surprise. How on earth he'd got here was just one more mystery in what had been the strangest period of his life to date. He found a side gate and stepped out into the street.

It was noon when he made his way into the courtyard where he lodged. As quietly as he could, he began climbing the stairs to his room. The fifth step creaked, as he forgot every time, and all at once, down in the hall where no landlady had been standing a second before, now stood Frau Trober. She was polishing the door knocker.

'That you, Herr Brahms?'

'Yes, I'm just going up to —'

'Weekend party, was it?'

'Well, I—'

'Must have been a good one.' She resumed rubbing.

He made a break for the next stair.

'By the way, Herr Brahms,' she called after him.

'Yes…?'

'The ceiling fell in on your room.'

'Oh…'

'Last night's rain. Clothes are all right, them as was in the wardrobe. Bed'll dry out. But all those papers…' She shook her head.

Brahms rushed the few steps back down to her. 'Papers? What about my papers?'

Frau Trober stood back from her door knocker and eyed it admiringly. 'There, come up a treat it has.'

The newly reconstituted composer stared at the devastation. Twenty years of symphonic scribbling, a trunkful of false starts, unconvincing developments and unresolvable codas lay scattered among lumps of plaster and ornamental moulding, the whole mess smeared and landlady-trampled into the squelch of sodden carpet. He picked up a fistful of suppurating music. Microwave it crisp and dry? What was the point? The ink had already run. He dropped the sopping wad on to the floor, and groaned.

The portraits looked on, but didn't offer a single word of sympathy. Well, he thought to himself, screw them.

This was the end.

He kicked a piece of ceiling across the room, and groaned again. He would have to move, he would have to begin all over again. But was it really worth it? He slumped backwards on to the sofa, and groaned for a third time.

The end, the end.

The end.

After a few moments he opened his eyes to gaze upwards. The lack of ceiling revealed, above it, a lack of roof. Parts of it remained, and elsewhere, where lines of tiles had been stripped by the wind, daylight was showing through. The effect, he thought to himself, was like gazing up at a celestial crossword puzzle, one that was without clues and for which there were no solutions. Just patches of darkness and lengths of blue sky...

He didn't know how long he remained there staring up into the meaningless and accidental pattern arching above him, but when he got to his feet at last, he felt strangely refreshed. He was *ready*.

With a clap of his hands that startled the portraits nearly out of their frames, he turned to the room and announced: 'New quill, new ink! New symphony! Ludwig Van B – R.I.P.!'

The fairy-tale science-fiction world of Antonin Dvořák

After turning several more pages of his illustrated *Fairy-Tales and Legends of Bohemia*, Dvořák had come to what was clearly a sweltering summer's day. The sun in the top right-hand corner of the sky looked too hot to touch; the rest was a cloudless wash of blue, flecked here and there with tick-marks for birds. Green swirls and straight up-and-down brown brushstrokes indicated a forest. The foreground, where he stood wiping the sweat from his brow, was strictly fairy-tale: a trail of breadcrumbs showed where the path lay, there was a carpet-of-flowers meadow, timorous deer, a babbling stream. Between the nearest trees – drawn in delicate pen and ink – lay a deepening darkness that ended as black night in the heart of the forest. A lonely charcoal burner's hut was sketched in near the bottom of the page. Any charcoal burner he'd ever read about had been morose. Why should this one be any different? He turned the page and kept going.

He was in good spirits. Last weekend he'd taken a major life decision. After years of producing traditional symphonies and quartets, he felt ready to move on. But move on to what, precisely? Was this merely a mid-life crisis? Fashionable *fin-de-siècle* blues? A few days taking time out to catch up on the historical shifts sweeping Europe, coupled with receiving the recent birthday-present book of fairy-tales (synchronicity, or what? he'd thought to himself) – and he knew exactly the kind of music he wanted to write.

Then came the stumbling-block.

He'd be exploring the remote Bohemian countryside, searching out the folk-tunes, rhythms and melodies that would provide a basis for his new work. Fine. But there would be no restaurants so far out in the sticks. He'd have to take his own food. Hence the stumbling-block: how to cook the picnic hamburgers and sausages in what were bound to be tinder-dry conditions? There'd be no question of lighting an open fire. A stumbling-block indeed.

He had almost given up the entire project when, that very morning, his local supermarket had come up trumps. Luckily it was a Thursday, Special Offer Day. One glance at the Special Offers counter – and he knew his worries were over. In time, every nationalist composer seeking to draw inspiration from his native countryside would come to look on his purchase as a methodological breakthrough. Afterwards, he'd filled his rucksack with local beer, and sausages and hamburgers from his father's old shop, then set off to explore the fairy-tales of Bohemia.

Having left the charcoal burner far behind, Dvořák now came to a magic well. He paused and looked down. If he climbed into the bucket and lowered himself to the very bottom, he knew he would probably come to another country...Frankly, he'd seen America and that too had been another country. A lick of the thumb, on to the next page and into the forest.

A dozen or so pages later, his stomach told him it was time for beer and sausages. He was ready for them. The forest was chill, damp and silent with heavy black ink shading, but a sneak peek ahead showed him sunlight breaking through the trees, and a hint of blue sky. Already the path was widening into a sunny clearing. Just the place for a picnic. He rubbed his hands: in no time at all, the sausages and hamburgers would be browning nicely, and the beer...

He turned the page, and stopped.

Or, more precisely, he was brought to a stop. A complete halt, in fact. Being an experienced reader of science fiction, Dvořák knew a force-field when he banged into one. His big toe had just stubbed itself against invisibility, and it hurt. He tried again. It hurt – again, just as much as the first time. He tested it with his fingertips, his hands, the tip of his nose; he rolled the side of his cheek against this unexpected nothingness.

For the next five minutes he examined the scene from every angle, turned the storybook upside-down, shook it even. Only when he'd made a complete circuit of the clearing, returning to the point he'd started from, did he grasp the full situation. Think positive, he told himself, he was merely being trapped *outside*, in the real world. A blank page – that was all he was being excluded from. No big deal. He was hungry enough, and thirsty. Thanks to his SF reading he knew the universe was a place where anything could happen at any time, anywhere – so why not an invisible force-field, and why not here and now? Anyway, it was time to eat. Maybe with some beer and a mixed grill inside him things would look different. He unstrapped his rucksack.

Ten minutes later the air around him was filled with the hiss-and-spit of partly done sausages and the sweet rancidity of sizzling hamburger. Yes, the decision he had taken last weekend was the right one: life as a late-nineteenth-century nationalist composer was, quite definitely, *the* life. Force-fields were interesting enough – but compared to abandoning time-hallowed symphonic form in favour of thematic textures arising directly from the harmonies and rhythms of his own homeland...even force-fields were nowhere. And the disposable barbecue had made it all possible.

He laughed to himself and had just begun whistling a *dumka* melody that had distinct orchestral possibilities when he heard a booming voice.

'ANTONIN DVOŘÁK!'

He glanced up from turning a sausage, but could see nothing.

The gloomy forest was still gloomy and everything else, force-field included, was pretty much as before. Wasn't it?

Well, not quite. As a child he'd once been given a magic painting book of blank pages – all he'd had to do was splash brushfuls of water over the paper to bring out the browns, greens and blacks of the inevitable enchanted-forest picture. Now, half a century later, it seemed that the process was being reversed: on all sides, starting from inside the force-field and working outwards, the forest colours seemed to be draining away. The gloomy twilight was turning grey, the grass, flowers and leaves were fading to a uniform paleness, the trees were smudges. Even more alarming: he'd started hearing voices.

To calm himself he bit into a sausage.

'ANTONIN DVOŘÁK!'

He stopped in mid-chew. The voice didn't seem to come from any one place, but as if from everywhere at once. A very bad sign.

'ANTONIN DVOŘÁK!'

To prove to himself he wasn't really frightened, he whistled his *dumka* melody, pretending it was fully orchestrated. Or he tried to – but in his anxiety he could only imagine it as chamber music, and that only for a few bars. Already, the outlines of the trees were becoming indistinct, his aluminium trough had begun flickering and growing insubstantial. Worst of all, the sausages and hamburgers had vanished altogether, leaving only smoke. Just when they seemed done to a turn, too.

Seriously alarmed, Dvořák got to his feet. Only, there was no longer any solid ground to stand on. None that he could see anyway. He took a few steps forward into thin air, into nothingness.

'Antonin Dvořák!'

The voice was coming from inside him now. 'Antonin Dvořák! Antonin Dvořák!...Antonin Dvořák!...Antonin Dvořák!...Antonin Dvořák!...'

As the words became fainter the consonants faded, then the vowels themselves began weakening...

'...Antonin Dvořák!...Antonin Dvořák !...Antonin Dvořák!...Antonin Dvořák!...!...ᴀᴀᴀᴀᴀᴀᴀᴏᴏᴏᴏᴏᴏᴏ........'

Nearer and nearer to silence. A silence phrased in the cadence of sighing, of longing and pleading. Silence, like the pause between heartbeats, or the still point when breathing-in has yet to become breathing-out…If he didn't do something, and pretty damn quick, Dvořák guessed he'd soon be silence himself. Silence standing in the middle of a completely blank page.

He began running back the way he'd come. Faster and faster he went. Blundering from side to side, trying his best to stay on the path or where he thought the path should be. Every few steps he bumped into the invisible trunks of invisible trees. When it was easier underfoot, he didn't know if he'd actually found the path or was simply going round in circles. Was there a critical point where apparent invisibility became complete nothingness? And had he passed it?

Is this what had happened to the likes of Liszt, Smetana and all the other composers who'd made the decision to ditch accepted symphonic form? Did transcending the conventional mean a disintegration of the familiar, turning this world into an anti-matter world? A negative domain? A black hole? He'd read all the SF books, knew all the SF terms – and didn't like any of them. He preferred it when everyone ended up safely back home on their own planet. Here, if he ever did reach an ending, would it have already disappeared? Or would the ending be the moment when he himself disappeared?

Finally he sat down. Exhausted. And bitterly disappointed. All he'd wanted was a pleasant stroll through some well-loved Bohemian fairy tales, a chance to set the modest groundwork for a nationalist school of music.

'ANTONIN DVOŘÁK!'

The voice was back.

He ignored it.

'ANTONIN DVOŘÁK!'

'Go away, will you!'

To his surprise the voice took the hint and went away. This time for good.

*

Dvořák was alone. Quite, quite alone in the middle of nowhere surrounded by nothing — an island adrift in unseen, unsounded waters, at the mercy of unknown currents and tides...

That was when the spirits of the deep emerged from between the empty particles, rising like a terrifying darkness out of the swirling nothingness around him. Spirits of evil, formless and boundless, pure force and elemental energy from the uncharted abyss. The Water Goblin, the Noonday Witch. Released from their confines like demons from the Nether World, like souls of the damned, they filled the air around him and ranged the trackless heavens, screeching, howling and tearing at the very fabric of Time and Space.

To Dvořák, a man who'd so recently shown the door to four-movement symphonic structure, these nightmare creatures were child's play. He turned and gave them a double-barrelled laser-type blast of his new creative vision:

Laser-type blast number one: from now on there would be one unbroken surge of melody, an unfolding tapestry of harmonic development
Laser-type blast number two: no concessions to sonata form.

Within moments the Water Goblin and the Noonday Witch had both conceded defeat. By the time The Wood Dove put in a belated appearance it was all over. Dvořák was a man triumphant: a master of all that was and of all that ever might be. Hearing the bird's solitary call, he looked up and addressed it in the tonal language of the century not yet begun. At once, its gentle-throated cooing became colour spilling across the unpainted sky, and from the beating of its outstretched wings there trailed a continuous rainbow dispensing true chromaticism upon the emptiness below. The blank pages were once again filling up with renewed life.

Exhausted, Dvořák fell to the ground.

*

Just over a century later a package tour (Ten Conferences in Ten Days) of musicologists, ethnologists and folklorists was passing through Old Bohemia. Confident that there was papers-material and to spare in that fairy-tale kingdom of enchanted castles, enough to make professors of them all, a splinter group of the most ambitious decided to take a day out. Though not princes in anyone's eyes, they were soon hacking a path through the tangled briars, brambles and weeds, with the single-minded determination of searchers after academic Chairs.

Finally they reached what they agreed must once have been a place of some significance. The remains of a disposable barbecue and the litter of empty beer bottles and sausage wrappers told of temporary habitation – a picnic spot, at the very least. Nearby, head resting on a rolled-up rucksack, someone was deeply asleep. Even close to, the man was mostly beard.

Espying a possible footnote, they naturally tried waking him. They prodded him, shouted and kicked. Nothing worked. At last one of them, the author of an ongoing, multi-volume analysis of *The Sleeping Beauty*, turned to his colleagues: 'Of course you know the only way to wake this guy?'

No further discussion was needed. Ambition will out. Though a few headed back along the path home, the rest sat down and, slightly embarrassed, waited for darkness to fall.

Haydn learns to put his demon to good use

'Yes?'

'...'

'And?'

'...'

'Really? And she wants – what?'

'...'

'*Who* did you say? Surely they didn't —'

'...'

'I'll think about it. Goodbye.' He rings off.

Haydn's symphonies occasionally give surges of violent emotion, but not the man himself. Not often, and not just now. He remains calm. He remains cool. He remains collected.

Yet he can hardly believe the phone call he has just had. His wife would like the two of them to appear on the *Jerry Springer Show* – is she mad? Having exhausted the emotional grunge of 'trailer trash', Rosanne the research-girl had explained to him, the producers decided to up the ratings by inviting well-known celebrities. Last week Kant was heckled into explaining why so few philosophers

– 57 –

got married. He was then proposed to, live on stage. He declined, and the audience nearly lynched him. A great start to a great show, she'd burbled. Next on was Fichte. His slot got off to a slow start, but once the audience grasped his theory of the Ego – that nothing *real* exists outside Fichte's own mind – they got verbal, then physical. Hard-core, knockabout stuff. The ratings soared.

The suggested script: that Haydn denounces his current mistress, then gets down on his knees to propose to his wife all over again. The show's seen by millions across North America and Europe, Rosanne pointed out. He'd get a night in a 5-star hotel and all travel expenses would be covered, including a limo to the studio. Tempting?

He's to call back by noon.

With cries of 'JER-RY! JER-RY! JER-RY!' ringing out like a low-budget chorus, he enters the music room and crosses over to the clavichord. The wooden floor creaks at every step. The stove's not been lit. The place is freezing.

Exposure on network TV would make his CDs a sell-out. Reissues, box-sets, mood anthologies. Celebrity status would guarantee him a seat on the gravy-train that runs back and forth between chat-shows, panel games and late night discussions about the arts. He'd be baryton-free for ever!

Yes, the *baryton*. That bane of his life. This morning especially.

His employer and patron, Prince Esterházy, wants a new baryton trio. Baryton trio number forty-seven – who cares? Haydn loathes the baryton. Cumbersome, dull, justly neglected. Maybe he should slip the prince one of the early ones, in a different key. His royal personage would never notice.

As Haydn sits down at the clavichord his chair creaks. His bones creak. In winter this part of the palace is an all-day icebox. He puts down his mobile and blows on his knuckles to warm them; his breath comes in clouds.

There are hours of grisly work ahead – he knows he should switch off his phone. But he doesn't; any interruption will be welcome. Also, he just can't bear to watch the tiny electronic hand waving 'goodbye' as it fades from the screen, not just now. It makes him feel as if he's being abandoned to his fate.

The room is so cold that when he shuts his eyes, he can almost pretend it's his day off and he's outdoors, wandering the windswept wastes of the Great Hungarian Plain. The middle of nowhere, but at least he'd be wrapped up warm! And having some *fun*: he and a few friends out hunting, with regular picnic-breaks of pies and schnapps. The early morning mist, the pale winter sky, chill sunlight. Perfect!

Not like this...

The clavichord is fragile-looking and fragile-sounding. When he opens the lid, the vibrating strings echo around the curtainless, carpetless, sub-zero room. A grim setting for the morning's grim task. Still half-dark too. He strikes the tinder box to make a spark, then reaches for the candle and lights it.

'It will be one of the great moments in western music.'

'Who said that?' He peers into the surrounding dimness.

'It's a premonition of the first performance of your oratorio *The Creation*. That great C major chord for full orchestra and chorus at the words: And there was LIGHT!'

Haydn whirls round in his seat: 'Where are you?'

The bleak room is empty. He's quite alone.

'Not yet though,' the voice continues. 'Not for another thirty years.'

'Show yourself. What do think you're —?'

Ignore it, he tells himself, *and it'll go away.*

'Even so, you have no time to waste pretending you're wandering windswept plains, eating pies and the rest of it. There's work to be done.'

'I know, I know!' Haydn grits his teeth and turns back to face the keyboard. Hearing voices? Just one more problem.

Like *The Jerry Springer Show*. 'Rousseau's already booked, *together*' – and here Rosanne had paused, with a laugh that sounded like breaking glass, to set up her punch-line – 'together with all the kids he's fathered and abandoned!'

Haydn shudders at the memory. But, he thinks to himself, why not? Financial independence for the rest of his life – in return for one brief act of televised self-debasement? Tempting isn't the word…

The moment calls for a reflective cigarette, if only to get the music room warmed up. And that's another thing. With that CD mega-payout, he could afford a house of his own with log fires burning in every room and limitless hot water. All for one hour's humiliation on cable, or less if you count the adverts.

Flip open the mobile. Check last caller. It's his old phone so he'll need to dial, then press the little green icon. Easy enough.

He punches the keys in time to a possible opening allegro of yet another symphony. His next one'll be number thirty-nine. He sighs. Thirty-nine! – how many more can there be?

'Sixty-five.'

It's in his ear, that's where the thing is. In his left ear!

'Come out of there!'

He cuts the call and puts down the phone. Then sets to fingering out the intruder.

'You'll end up with over eighty quartets, fifty-three piano sonatas —' The voice is getting a little breathless and muffled as it retreats into the whorls.

Haydn's finger digs deeper.

'Twelve concertos for piano, concertos for *lira organizzata*, for violin, cello, trumpet, forty-seven piano trios, not to mention all the operas, masses, cantatas and oratorios.' The cataloguing ends in a rush. 'Don't worry, though, I'll help you.' A soothing croon of a voice, viola-coloured.

He removes his finger. 'What do you mean – *help* me?'

Silence.

Haydn jumps to his feet. 'What am I *doing*? Who do I think I'm talking to? My left ear? I'm going mad, that's what it is. Mad. Mad. Mad.'

He sits down again. He's reaching for his mobile when…

A dirge-like scraping has begun somewhere in the inner labyrinth of his left ear. Dirge-like, and baryton-like.

Yes, he's going out of his mind. He must be.

He tells himself: stay calm, stay cool, stay collected…

…and watch your right hand stretching forwards, opening the ink pot, picking up the quill. Dipping it in. Your other hand's pulled over a sheet of music-paper.

He shakes his head. It's not really happening. Can't be.

Ignore it. Ignore everything. Phone *The Jerry Springer Show*. It's your only hope. Get yourself out of here – out of this asylum!

His hand with the quill has now begun to write out what looks like a line of crochets and quavers.

It's one baryton trio too many – and the pressure's finally got to you. The proof? You're watching your hand sketch out a bass-line under instructions coming from your left ear?

Yes, he's really losing it.

Time to get out of here. Phone Jerry Springer and —

It's getting worse. He can't believe what he's seeing now: the melody line's coming next. Note after note – getting rapidly inked in, right before his very eyes.

Fine, fine, fine, he tells himself. That's it. You're going off your head.

Clutching the phone, like a drowning man. Flip it open. Redial. It's ringing…

But he just can't resist a glance down to see what kind of music his madness is producing. Melody line above, bass line below, and not all crazy and blotchy as he's expecting, but neat, clear and ordered. The movement – an undemanding allegro in 2/4 time – has *Thump-thump-Thumpity-thump*ed its way through a series of straightforward tonic-dominant chords, and come to a merciful stop.

New bar-line, new movement. Same key.

Meanwhile, in the Jerry Springer office, someone's answered. Haydn clears his throat: 'Can I speak to Rosanne in research, please?'

'…'

'Yes, I'll wait.'

Glancing down again, he can see the trio's coming along rather nicely.

'...'

'Joseph Haydn here.'

'...'

'Joseph Haydn, the composer. I want to speak to Rosanne, please. She asked me to call her back to arrange —'

'...'

'I've already been waiting for over —'

'Finished,' interrupts the voice in his left ear.

'Pardon?'

'Finished, I said. Baryton trio number 47. With enough note-for-note repeats to avoid over-taxing the royal fingers. A doddle.'

His other ear: 'Rosanne speaking. Well, Joe – are we going for it? Your wife —'

Haydn closes the mobile, puts it carefully down on the polished wood surface of the clavichord. He stares at the newly written music. A trio sonata in less than ten minutes?

Easy-to-play, predictable, with hardly an inspired note from beginning to end. Perfect. The Prince – who has a lot more enthusiasm than talent – will love it. Amazing.

Miraculous.

He manages a nod of appreciation. Adding that he couldn't have done better himself.

'My pleasure —' comes the reply, 'and I'll write the others too, if you like.'

'What others?'

'The other seventy-nine trios still to come.'

'There are *seventy-nine* more!' The prospect of banality on such a scale almost takes Haydn's breath away. He pauses, then adds: 'Would you? Would you really?'

'Certainly, as and when required.'

'But – why *would* you? Why would anyone?'

'Trust me.'

'But —? I just don't understand.'

Haydn is hoping for a few words of reassurance. A bargain of some sort being struck, perhaps. A reason that makes sense. Any reason. But none is offered.

'Trust me – that's all I ask.'

The candle's burned down to a hiss and spit. It goes out. Cold winter-light takes possession of the room once more. Haydn shivers.

Time to roll up the music-paper in preparation for the journey ahead. He must make his way along corridor after draughty corridor, up and down staircase after forlorn staircase, across courtyards and cobbles, through state rooms, reception rooms and ballrooms, to come at last into the royal antechamber. The Royal Presence. After a humble lowering of the head and some deferential words of greeting he'll seat himself at the keyboard ready to give his ever-diplomatic accompaniment to the princely scrapings.

He leaves the music room humming the leaden theme of the third movement, with its dismal adagio introduction. Soon the modestly talented bow will be going *saw-saw-saw* across the main strings of the baryton while the others drone in sympathy...

Ta-UM, ta-UM, ta-UM...

His demon's whispering to him how one day, and to the same carefully measured pace, four bearers will carry him shoulder-high on his chair into a performance of *The Creation*. Their fragile and precious burden of skin, bone and exhaustion will raise a hand in acknowledgement as polite society applauds the entrance of 'Papa' Haydn. He is their servant, elevated. His last appearance in public: he will lean his wasted arms on the plump upholstery of the chair, anticipating that glorious C major chord.

The corridor's unheated, of course. He might as well be halfway along a frozen river. Pausing for a moment, he inclines his head to marvel at a flight of imaginary geese high above him. A flawless formation, each perfectly synchronised beat of their wings growing steadily louder and louder and...almost sounding like *JER-RY! JER-RY! JER-RY*

'Some chance!' he remarks to the footman, who's opening the double-door ahead.

His mobile again. He stops to answer it. Young Wolfgang – wondering if there's to be a get-together next Sunday to play through a few new pieces.

'You betcha!' replies Haydn. 'Be there, or be square!'

'You'll have another quartet by then,' whispers the voice he knows only too well, 'and you'll have entered your *Sturm und Drang* period.'

Haydn reaches up to have another poke at his demon, an affectionate one this time.

'Why not?' he says out loud. 'Why not have a *Sturm und Drang* period? Everybody else does.' With that, he hurries off to keep his appointment with the Prince.

The footman shakes his head and sets a puff of powder rising light, fine and halo-like into the air. He remarks to the empty corridor: 'These eighteenth-century composers – what are they *on*?'

Mozart tries out a major career move

Wolfgang sat down, rolled a cigarette and began to make plans. A few moments ago he'd told his father he'd written his very last contredanse for the Archbishop and had had it with wigs, breeches and batons. He was going to be a private detective, a shamus. Leopold had said nothing, but turned on his heels and marched straight out the door. Which said it all.

The ex-composer blew a perfect smoke ring and gazed into it. Yes, surely there was more to life than sitting two places down from the cook at the servants' table and grinding out endless cassations, divertimenti and serenades like some eighteenth-century muzak-monkey. Out of sheer habit a few minutes later, he found himself humming the possible opening bars of a new symphony. He decided to call it K183.

'No! No! No!' he shouted aloud. He was going to be a private eye. Starting right *now*.

He stood up, wrenched off his wig and drop-kicked it across the room. No more symphonies for him, no more concertos, no more K numbers. But the more he tried to picture himself tracking down stashed loot, doing tail jobs, following a paper trail of numbered accounts to the Cayman Islands, discovering bodies in trunks and putting the squeeze on blackmailers – the more K183 just seemed to keep on coming: the exposition of first and second subjects, the development, recapitulation, coda. Perfect sonata form.

Meanwhile, darkness was falling. Soon crime would begin to stalk the streets of Salzburg. This was no time for thinking – he had to *do* something. Luckily enough, he'd caught a *film-noir* retrospective on cable recently and knew exactly what was needed.

The makeover took a few hours, but was worth the effort. He ditched the *ancien-régime* decor and went strictly retro: neon strip-lighting, Venetian blinds, a hat-stand, roll-top desk, swivel chair and filing cabinet. Lastly, he fitted a glass panel to his door and stencilled the words: W. A. MOZART – PRIVATE EYE. He laughed to himself: the Archbishop's reception was going to be a few contredanses short that evening…

He had just sat down to roll another cigarette when he became aware of a silhouette darkening the glass panel. For nearly a full minute nothing more happened: someone was clearly having difficulty reading the gothic script. All at once, the door burst open and a man – brimmed hat, belted trench coat, bullet wound through the heart – fell into the room. He was carrying a bulky package.

The following Sunday, and for probably the very last time, Wolfgang made the journey to Vienna and the weekly get-together at Van Swieten's. It was good to be among friends once more. Haydn, Vanhal and Ditters were hard-headed composers of the First Viennese School: they could be counted on to fulfil any contract, any commission: from sonatinas to symphonies, with or without a minuet, and same-day turn-around. Haydn had brought a new string quartet for them to play through; they examined some Bach fugues with a view to arranging them as string trios for the following week. They all had a good belly-laugh at the new-wave of *galant* composers who regarded fugues like these as old-fashioned. Old-fashioned? – they were timeless. As the afternoon wore on, Wolfgang realised how much he was going to miss this kind of friendly banter.

Finally, over the usual Chinese carry-out and wine, he told them about his new career. They were surprised. He moved quickly on to describe his new office furniture, his first dead client and the package which had proved to contain an assortment of tapes, CDs and accompanying promotion-packs. Then he selected a CD, invited them to fill their glasses, sit back, and listen.

Track one was short.

Afterwards there was a long, long silence. Wolfgang took this opportunity to hand round the sleeve-notes. Van Swieten, their faithful page-turner and host, hovered with his customary deference at the edge of their little circle as if the charge set up by their combined creativity might overload him. He was a modest man. After a nervous cough, he asked, 'This *Stockhausen*...he is a great composer too, like you?'

'Well,' Wolfgang drawled in his newly acquired drawl, then opened one of the explanatory manifestos: 'Says here that Stockhausen's music is written for the Post-Apocalypse.'

'Which one?' Van Swieten paused, glancing into the future to tick off the French Revolution, various colonial and post-colonial genocides, two world wars, Vietnam, the Twin Towers...then he blinked as though to clear from his sight the horrors that were yet to come. He coughed again, 'Let's play some more Bach.'

But his well-meaning suggestion went unheard, drowned out by the opening discords of track two: a Boulez piano sonata. It was a compilation album.

Hours later, as Wolfgang was pedalling home to Salzburg through the darkness, he did his best to recapture something of his initial excitement at his new career. But no matter how hard he tried, the conclusion was always the same: if being a private eye meant putting up with the likes of Stockhausen, Boulez and Cage – then forget it.

The night was clear and cold. Within moments of setting off, he'd found himself composing to keep warm, continuing K183 at the point where he'd left it that fateful morning. Soon he was well into the last movement allegro. As the G minor allegro turned to molto vivace, he pedalled to keep up with it. Hard work: the road was anything but an autobahn, as every pothole and rut reminded him. But then, while he neared the fourth movement coda — his legs creating a brilliant Catherine-wheel effect with his shoe-buckles glittering in the moonlight — the strangest thing happened.

At first he thought he'd run into the back of some cart or coach travelling without its lights on, or else had hit a pothole and was about to take a header over the handlebars. But no. He was starting to rise into the air.

Then he rose higher, and higher.

Of course he had to keep pedalling. Having finished K183, he went straight on to K184. The Austrian countryside lay further and further below. Here and there a light showed in an isolated farmhouse; the dark patches were fields, the darker ones forest; everything as though engraved upon the sheen of moonlight. The road had all but disappeared. K184 completed, he quantum-leaped eighty-seven K numbers in one overwhelming burst of inspiration straight to the concerto in E flat, K271. A glimpse of the river unwinding below, like a thread of unpolished silver, had shown him the line of the entire piano part at a glance. This, set in the shifting orchestral tones of the darkened landscape, would guide him safely home.

Though riding a bike is a skill never forgotten, aerial cycling is trickier. So long as he kept pedalling out masterpiece after masterpiece, he felt he could stay aloft for ever. Initial judders and overbalancings had been corrected and now he glided confidently through the night. All around was complete silence save for an occasional breath of wind, the pleasing rush of well-oiled chain over sprocket, the whirring spokes. His footwork powered him towards the development section.

The kilometres sped by, and so too did the K numbers. He continued his effortless way ever onwards and upwards. Ahead he could see the lights of Salzburg where he would have to drop speed and bring himself gradually down to land. In less than a quarter-hour, he'd be wheeling his bike round to the stables next to the Archbishop's palace. Then it would be off with the bicycle clips and back to scratching out contredanses.

Irritation took hold, and a sense of the injustice of it all. Forget his career move. It had been a wash-out. Forget Stockhausen. He pedalled harder than ever, and rose again. His new-found fluency and grace and elegance sent him soaring up high above the city and upward through more unwritten Ks. Finally, as had Giotto, he described an unbroken flow of mastery and precision in air. He had reached the slow movement of his piano sonata K280. He ceased pedalling. Yet, such was his perfection of poise and balance, that bicycle and rider remained as though weightless, tracing out a perfect circle high above the provincial capital. Gradually, stars visible and invisible fell under the spell of his supreme and wordless utterance. From nearest to furthest, constellations and galaxies, white dwarfs and red giants gathered round him, rearranging themselves and the entire heavens in harmony with this perfectly created moment. For one brief instant, all creation was hushed – and affirmed.

When the last note could be sustained no longer and had faded once more into the infinite darkness, Wolfgang resumed pedalling. It had been a glorious moment, and it had passed. He shrugged, and smiled to himself: he knew there would be others. He was happy.

Dawn was breaking a short time later as he brought down his machine to land safely on the empty courtyard of the palace. There was no one around to hear the wheels scrunching the gravel as he made his way to the stables. Having put away his bicycle, he stood and watched first light come slanting over the fields and woods; it was bringing him new contredanses, new serenades and cassations. It was bringing him a new day.

Schubert and the magic business card

The scene: Vienna. The time: autumn 1828, two months before Schubert's tragically early death at the age of thirty-one. As if he knows that his time is running out, the young composer has decided to take up a new hobby: now, thanks to his skateboard, he can get around the city much faster. He is the only splash of colour across the faded sepia print of old Vienna. Darting this way and that among the broughams and landaus, swerving crouched down between the legs of the plumed horses, cutting in front of merchants' carts and doing his best to avoid the invisible squad cars of Metternich's secret police – watch him go!

All that stops him soaring into a double-flip-and-roll above the spires of the Altstadt is the heavy rucksack strapped to his back: it's stuffed with lieder, unpublished symphonies, unheard operas, unsung masses and unplayed sonatas. And today there's something new in there, something very, very special.

A Schubertiad at four o'clock, and he's late. A final skid round the corner into von Spaun's courtyard, a jaw-juddering rattle over the last stretch of cobbles, a final jolt – and stop. Skateboard under his arm, he walks in, grinning: earlier that day it had seemed there might be no more Schubertiads and no more Schubert, ever.

He'd been woken by his room cracking apart in sudden heat. Having sat up in bed he'd stared at the gaping sky above, the buildings stacked jaggedly on either side like so many tumbled packs of cards. Still dreaming? He leaped out of bed and waited to see what would happen next. This, he told himself, was surely just another day getting started. Most days began more or less the same. This one didn't, that was all. Give it time.

And until then? Should he stand there in his nightshirt, nightcap and socks till the rest of Creation got its act together?

So, maybe dreaming or maybe not…

From across the rubble lying heaped between him and the street below came the heat of a summer's day. Not a First Viennese School summer, however, nor even equatorial, this one rose straight and scorching from the earth's core. Brightness bleached of all colour, blinding harshness. The heavy baroque masonry, the squares and avenues, the statues, the urns along the rooftops, the unshuttered balconies, the whole imperial capital in fact, was shimmering and simmering, and almost at combustion point. His floor was trackless flame, his walls cascading incandescence.

All at once, his furniture – the bed, the washstand, the piano, the desk, the chair, the vats of ink and limitless music-paper, which had been rearranging itself, skipping from spot to spot to stay cool or at the very least avoid catching fire – vanished altogether. As did his apartment, the nearby streets and the entire city of Vienna itself. Nothing remained except the burning beneath him and the distant cries of souls in torment.

'What a fucking start to the day!' thought Schubert.

By sheer effort of creative will, he began drawing out the remaining shreds of this dying world, coaxing them, stroking them into sound. At his touch, the chaos whirling around him steadied, taking on the faintest outline and a rhythm faltering at every step. Though all had seemed lost until then, there now came the hint of a slow-paced, heartbreaking waltz. Every emergent note was like a blessing.

*

Since leaving his house and skateboarding through the streets of Vienna to Von Spaun's, he has been aware of the andante from his new Piano Sonata in A Major glowing to itself in the darkness of his rucksack; all the way over town he's felt it warming his back. Now that he's arrived, it has cooled down to near playing-temperature. He can't help whistling the opening bars as he makes his way along the corridor to the crowded reception room.

And here they all are: von Spaun, Mayrhofer, Vogl and the rest of the gang. A plate of snacks, a table of uncorked reds – some still breathing, others already dead men – and a rack of discount Cava in the fridge. The evening begins: Vogl announces that while everyone waits for the barbecue coals to whiten, he and Schubert will run through a few favourites from the lieder-cycles.

A newcomer is seen to shake his head: 'Lieder-cyles? They won't get you a penthouse with a pool on the roof.'

Who's asking *him*? Odd-looking guy in a cape, cord trousers and beige Hush-Puppies, as if he'd dressed in the dark. At Schubertiads everyone does something: a bit of poetry, piano-playing, singing, juggling, whatever. So, apart from sticking his oar in, what can Herr Hush-Puppy do that's wonderful?

'You'd like a pool on the roof, wouldn't you?'

Schubert gives a modest shrug. 'People are kind. I have a room, a bed, a washstand, a piano, a desk, a chair, vats of ink and limitless music-paper. What more could I need?' He reaches for an early *wurst*. 'I can only be in one room at a time and when I want to see the world, I have my skateboard. Life is good.'

'It could be better.'

'If I am creating, I am happy.'

'Hard work, creating.'

Briefly he remembers his recent descent into hell to come back with the morning's andante. Hard work, right enough. 'Yes, but good work.' He lays out the score of *Winterreise,* planning to start with the lieder-cycle heavies then lighten things up by barbecue-time.

Herr Hush-Puppy follows him over to the piano: 'Remember Diabelli's response to the A Minor Sonata you sent him a few years

back? "Too difficult and gloomy. How about a few beginners'
studies?" Remember that?'

Herr Hush-Puppy must have hacked into the publisher's
records. Who the fuck is this guy to go on about his rejections?
He'd been waiting months for Diabelli's reply, waiting and hoping
right up to that very moment when the weighty slap on the
doormat told him the bad news. Sometimes it seems he's spent his
whole life waiting. And for what? Rejections, or invitations to
compose for four-year-olds. He's not sure which is worse.

Drawing himself up to his full five foot nothing, he demands:
'Your point, sir?'

'Just making conversation, Franz. I may call you Franz, Franz?'

Schubert says nothing.

'My card.' Herr Hush-Puppy hands him a business card.

It's completely blank. Schubert turns it over. The other side's
just as blank.

'Fill in the details to suit,' comes the explanation. 'Whoever
you feel you have need of the most, that's who I'll become.'

'Are you some telegram/kissogram kind of thing?'

No response.

Schubert looks down at the man's dated footwear: 'Are you the
Devil?'

'You would like me to be?' asks the stranger eagerly. 'Nothing
simpler, and never any shortage of role models!'

The composer ignores him and sits down at the piano. Vogl takes
up position, Schubert gives him an A, and the evening begins.

The hours pass in a dizzying whirl of lieder-cycles, new
sonatas, new four-handed piano works, poems about tragic love,
despair and suicide; there are *wurst*-breaks and wine-breaks. By
midnight the barbecue's a heap of ash and the Cavas are all
finished. Schubert's heading for his skateboard when Herr Hush-
Puppy appears at his side: 'Remember, Franz, that card is *your*
card, and yours alone. Don't squander it. I don't give out cards to
just anyone.'

'But why me?' Secretly the young composer is sure he's about to be told he's a neglected genius, and that it's high time the world gave him the recognition he deserves. He prepares to shift into bashful-modesty mode.

'Because you're cute!' comes the answer.

Over the next few days Schubert takes out the business card every so often and examines it. A sartorially distressed fairy godmother or guardian angel like Herr Hush-Puppy will solve all his problems? Really? What's the catch? Nobody hangs around Schubertiads dishing out free offers unless they're after something. Schubert's tried tearing the card, biting it, setting fire to it. The thing's indestructible. He's tried throwing it away, losing it, tossing it over the edge of a cliff then skateboarding away as fast as he can – only to arrive home and find it propped up on his mantelpiece. When he returned from flushing it three times in a row down the Bahnhof Superloo one morning, it was waiting for him, in the same place as always, and not even damp.

He's become obsessed. He hardly sleeps anymore, and when he does he dreams about the card: one night, it becomes a communion-wafer swollen to the size of his mattress and he's being forced to swallow it; on another, it has turned into a magic carpet floating high above the city, the magic's running out and he's begun to fall...

A month later, after a few more masterpieces have been brought into an uncaring world, Schubert goes for an afternoon's recreational skateboarding. He's enjoying himself swishing about the streets, stitching in and out between the traffic, alarming the pedestrians in the Prater. His only concession to public safety is a warning cry, in waltz-time: '*Haydn, then Mozart, Beet-hoven then me!*' His round glasses flash in the Viennese sunlight. Every few minutes he imagines he's caught sight of Herr Hush-Puppy and goes whizzing up to complete strangers: a circus midget, a female traffic warden, a lollipop-man. How could he be so mistaken?

Several women complain. One tells him to come back once he's got himself a real car.

Finally he's had it. He brakes to a sudden halt in the street. Out with the business card. Out with the biro. *Whoever you feel you have need of the most, that's who I'll become.*

A deep breath to cover his embarrassment. Then Schubert fills in the blank. And waits.

Maybe there'll be a puff of smoke to announce the stranger's arrival, or the earth will cleave in two at his feet, or the heavens part?

Maybe…He continues to wait, and wait. There's no smoke, no cleaving, no parting. Nothing. There's only the empty street. And himself. And his skateboard.

He'll give it another five minutes.

Still nothing.

He's taken out the business card again to check.

What he had written a few moments ago in his nervous, shaky handwriting is still there. He reads it over to himself, out loud.

Suddenly he's aware that Herr Hush-Puppy is standing right in front of him.

'But how – how did you get…?'

'By bus.' The stranger indicates the 41A he's just stepped from, its cheerful logo, body-lines, chassis and wheels growing rapidly fainter and indistinct. 'I had a sudden hunch you needed me, and had my Saver day-ticket all ready.'

'But I don't understand…' Schubert falls silent as he watches the now almost transparent bus vanish completely.

'So, how can I help you?'

Schubert is about to hand over the card when the stranger stops him: 'You can change your mind if you want. This is your last chance. Make no mistake, once I have my instructions I *will* carry them out.'

'Suits me.'

The man pockets the card: 'I'll be in touch.'

'But don't you want to look at it?'

'All in good time, Franz. Now you have inscribed your future, as it were, there is no rush. It will happen. I, in the manner you have commanded, will make it happen.'

Schubert is about to interrupt when Herr Hush-Puppy holds up his hand for silence: 'Although my appearance doubtlessly seems the same, there is already a re-scrambling, a reconfiguring going on inside me. Cells are dividing, conjoining; chromosomes reassembling themselves. This can happen slowly or quickly. Had you requested the Devil...or God, say, or an angel or demon, the process would take only a matter of moments. A rearrangement of priorities, merely.'

'But —' Schubert's getting exasperated, 'You've not even glanced at the damn thing. You're a fraud. To think of all the time I've wasted...'

'Glancing at it is the last thing I do, but I do indeed do it! Never fear!' The stranger smiles. 'Rather, even now I am sensing its non-verbal dynamics, what I call its *significant* data: the pressure of your hand when you wrote, the angle of the letters, the evidence of hope, of longing, need, the whole physiognomy of your soul as revealed at the instant of your writing. The words themselves are a mere by-product, at best a confirmation of your intentions. You with me?'

'Confirmation? But surely —'

'And sometimes not even that, for I can tell when a writer is in error. By the nature and degree of the discrepancy between what has been written and the significant data, I deduce the writer's real intentions — intentions often hidden even from himself. Then try to correct as best I can and set him — shall I say? — on his true course.'

'So it doesn't matter a fuck what I wrote?'

'If that's how you wish to interpret it...Ah, but here's a 41A. Please excuse me.'

'What? I – Wait —'

'Bye!'

'Bloody crackpot! Bampot! CHAR-LA-TAN!' Relishing the shout-qualities of the word 'Charlatan!' he shouts it several more times.

With Herr Hush-Puppy gone, the world seems an emptier place. Schubert remains at the street corner. He feels lost, abandoned. His future, which he'd been focusing on, heart and soul, for the last month, now seems – like the 41A – to have vanished into nothingness. His foot in position, he begins to roll the skateboard up and down the immediate stretch of pavement, moodily. Up the street, down the street: neither way leads anywhere, not any more. He gives the board a last shove and hops on: 'Fuck it, and fuck him!'

There's to be a Schubertiad in the evening, the last that Schubert will ever attend. A four p.m. kick-off, with the pizza-delivery booked for seven. It's been a month since the previous get-together. Bampots aside, life goes on.

Having crossed the city in a virtuoso blur of launches, half-pipes and jumps, Schubert skateboards straight in the front door at von Spaun's, along the corridor and into the main reception room. With a dexterous kick-flip he sends the board spinning into the air and catches it. There's a smattering of applause. He takes a bow.

Rucksack off, music unpacked; he reaches for a couple of quick *wurst* and a beer to keep him going until pizza-time. A chat with his host about who's playing what, then he glances over to the piano…

There, by herself in front of the keyboard, ready to be invited to turn the pages perhaps, sits a girl. A young woman. Is she beautiful? Is she dark, or fair? Tall? Petite? Full-figured? Slim? GSOH? Likes nights out and evenings in? Walking and pets? Though Schubert gazes and gazes at her, if he was given a questionnaire he couldn't even begin to tick the appropriate boxes, or any box at all.

His *wurst* are forgotten.

He's aware of Mayrhofer standing beside him. 'Didn't quite catch her name, I'm afraid. Came by herself, but she said someone had invited her.' After a pause he adds, 'Unusual shoes.'

Schubert doesn't answer.

Just at that moment, the girl glances up. She smiles at him.

The last autumn that Schubert will ever know is coming to its close; he has only a few weeks of life remaining. He smiles back at the girl. He's shy with girls. The air has a sudden chill in it, like a draught from an open window. He shivers, then makes as if to glide over to her – realising only too late that he's no longer standing on his skateboard.

Awkwardly, he takes a first step towards certain happiness.

Travelling via San Francisco and the moon: seven days in the life of Robert Schumann

Robert Schumann was in his mid-twenties when he awoke one morning to find Leipzig had become a town in provincial China (Late Tang). Standing at his bedsit window he gazed across the rooftops to the outskirts of the city. His heart lifted at the sight of the pagodas, the conical hats, the rickshaws, gongs and noodle stalls. Most of all he relished the mist wreathing the inaccessible mountain peaks far in the distance and the swirl of Chinese brushwork characters that decorated the right-hand side of the sky.

Sensing that the oriental motif wouldn't last for long, he dressed quickly and hurried outdoors. Downtown, he wandered here and there, admiring the lotus-pool courtyards, the temples and holy shrines. Time off like this made him feel a little guilty – he was determined upon a career as a concert pianist. His determination went far beyond study and practice. For example, he had passed up on marriage to the young and pretty Ernestine, knowing her illegitimacy would hardly be a good career move. Determination, in a big way.

Overwhelmed by the mysteries and exotic splendours of the Orient, he was soon drawn (call it Fate, call it curiosity) into a curio-seller's basement shop.

The doorbell chimed the whole-tone scale as he stepped into a twilight world of incense, heavy silks and lacquer-box darkness. His eyes growing accustomed to the dimness, he became aware of an elderly man shuffling towards him, hands clasped in front, marsupial-like, in the folds of his robe.

'Yes?'

Robert: 'Just looking.'

'Looking, yes.' The owner attended with a calmness appropriate to his dress and cultural epoch while Robert blundered his way among the delicacy of tables and porcelain, examining jade Buddhas, peering into teapots.

'You are seeking…?'

Without Robert's having heard a sound, the owner had approached and was standing at his side.

'Yes, I'm looking for…'

But what was he looking for? He had a piano, a promising career as a nineteenth-century piano virtuoso, and his *Neue Zeitschrift für Musik* journal allowed Florestan and Eusebius, as he called the two opposing sides of his artistic nature, to agree and disagree (getting himself paid twice over). Moreover, his tendency to melancholia frequently passed for profundity. So why had he come into the shop?

'For this, perhaps?' The curio-seller was holding out what looked like a spring-loaded nutcracker. 'Allow me.'

When Robert lifted his eyes from the contraption fitted to his hand, it was as if he were seeing everything around him as an image on disturbed water. Ripple upon ripple crossed the surface of the dimly lit basement shop, making the ornaments and bric-a-brac sway…Finally everything settled and he found himself standing in front of a soberly dressed, nineteenth-century Leipzig shopkeeper who was concluding his sales pitch: 'Next to you, sir, concert pianists the likes of Hummel, Moscheles, Kalkbrenner and Cramer will sound like mere vampers.'

'Vampires?'

Being a Romantic composer in an era recently dominated by Gothic fiction, Robert was easily confused. The misunderstanding resolved, the determined music maestro parted with cash and left.

Unfortunately, determination, like ambition, just can't sit back and let things fall into place. It must be up and tampering. Robert was no sooner home than he began fiddling with the nutcracker-looking thing: tightening it here, stretching it there, adjusting it, taking it apart...Finally he decided to sleep on it, literally. He fastened it round his fingers as he'd been shown and then snuggled under the blankets to let this miracle of mechanical ingenuity take its course. Which it did.

A week later, Robert returned from seeing the doctor, who'd confirmed that the damage done to the tendons of his fingers was quite irreversible. So much for mechanical ingenuity, and so much for his concert career. The Leipzig weather sympathised: the sky shifted between slate-grey and bruise-black and back to grey again, sagging clouds leaked mist and drizzle. Four o'clock in the afternoon, a hormonal low point as Robert well knew. He sat at his piano and stumbled through a few scales and riffs. But really, what was the point?

Leipzig's architectural moods were usually at one with his own. Not today though. The previous day's Stalinist building slabs would have been perfect, but they had already faded to a modernism of glass and steel. A see-through democracy of sliding doors, mirror-effect ceilings, walls of cascading water, conveyor-belt corridors, moving staircases and external lifts with panoramic views across the city: the New Germany that greeted him as he stepped outdoors made him feel even worse.

And it wasn't just the unaccustomed traffic lights, tram rails and bus lanes. In less than an hour he had to give a piano lesson at

Herr Wieck's Pianoforte Emporium. Till then he planned to be silent and withdrawn, whatever the current architecture. When Bach had been choirmaster at the Leipzig Thomaskirche, the harassed composer had often been driven to beat time by bouncing the pastor's pulpit-bible (Old *and* New Testaments) on the heads of badly behaved schoolboy choristers. Robert's teaching contract with Herr Wieck denied him any such therapeutic relief, and the strain was beginning to tell.

Herr-Wieck, Herr-Wieck. Left-right, left-right. He paced out the man's name, treading it into the pavement, stamping it down at every step. *Herr-Wieck, Herr-Wieck, Herr-Wieck.*

Just then he saw a flight of steps going underground. He knew just how they felt. Suited him. He went on the Inner Circle and stayed there until it was time for his lesson. But had he known what was waiting for him at Herr Wieck's, he would no doubt have got off at the next stop and jet-packed himself right to the door.

At five he was in the Wieck drawing-room, in the apartment above the piano shop. From below came sounds of would-be purchasers giving the selection of keyboards a test-drive. Snatches of Schubert, some Beethoven…To Robert this was but a background. Background number one, let's call it.

Close to was background number two: Herr Wieck himself, an assemblage of hands and shoulders jerking with emphasis and a head nodding, sometimes with a nod of urgency, sometimes a nod of caution. There was a mouth that opened and closed, opened and closed. Probably it was saying something. Robert didn't care.

He saw only Clara, Herr Wieck's daughter. From that moment on, as the song has it, she was in his thoughts, in his dreams, her face looked up at him from the empty plate when he'd eaten all his *kalbshaxe und kartoffelstock*. Clara gave a glow to the Leipzig sunshine and came down, as it were, with the Leipzig rain.

No longer likely to make his fortune as a piano virtuoso, what Robert saved on chocs and flowers he lavished on music paper and ink. He began to deluge the pretty young pianist (a rose-petal seventeen to his sturdy oak of twenty-seven) with piano miniatures of his own composition. A sonata followed, intimate piano duets with generous writing for crossed hands. Being shy as well as short of cash, he expressed his longing in staves and crochets, in time signatures and bar lines. Clara played the piano rather well.

Herr Wieck knew a lost cause when he saw one, and he could see that Robert had LOST CAUSE stamped right across his forehead. From starting out as a promising virtuoso the young man had turned himself into, pianistically speaking, a broken finger. All her short life Clara had been undergoing parental grooming, and moulding; now, after ten years, she was pretty much groomed, moulded and set. A proper concert pianist; not prodigy jailbait, but genuine talent and musical integrity. Herr Wieck was ready to take on Europe, and clean up.

Naturally he forbade the lovers to meet. At this, Leipzig ceased its architectural frivolity and hardened to a rigid masonry of stone walls, slates, shutters, iron railings and cobbled streets. Day became night, and there existed only ten minutes' radiance per twenty-four hours. At precisely six p.m. each evening – and with several streets between them – Robert would sit down at his bedsit upright and Clara at her family grand: they would play the same piece.

Love conquered all. They married. They moved to Dresden.

Then to Düsseldorf.

Previous cities may have had the sensitivity to accommodate to his changing moods, but from the day he arrived in Düsseldorf, Robert could see that this particular city was in a state of near disintegration. He alone seemed aware of it; he alone could hold it all together.

Tuesday evening. In a few minutes he would be leaving to go and conduct the local choir. Clara had already packed the music he'd be needing; his leather music-case was on the table. She had sent the children out of the room and was talking to him. Much as he wanted to listen to her he could not risk shifting his concentration to take in her exact words. Instead, he followed the melodic line of her voice. The encouragement, the sympathy and, most of all, the love. In the midst of the urban collapse around him, this loving cadence was something clear and definite to hold on to. Something strong and certain.

Out in the hall the clock chimed the quarter-hour.

'Robert?'

But he was already standing up, wasn't he? Walking towards her, giving her a kiss on the cheek and saying that he felt fine and that he'd be back at ten. He had certainly intended to say these things...Concentrate, he told himself, you have to concentrate. Don't allow yourself a moment's distraction. Touch the back of her hand to reassure her, and smile. Now go.

Outside, you button up your coat. Darkness comes in slices, a street-width. Who can tell what lies beyond it? The pavement cracking beneath your feet at every step, the walls splitting open, the sounds of glass breaking, of doors banging emptily, the night sky torn across from side to side, hanging in tatters...

Finally you reach the church hall. You put down your leather case. You watch the members of the Düsseldorf choir getting themselves into position. A late arrival has come in through the side door, disturbing the candle flames and making the room itself tremble and flicker. It settles again, safely. Herr Tausch...of course. The man's coming up to you. Naturally he is. With his outstretched hand, his smile and that voice of his pitched between anxiety and concern. A scheming man worthy only of your contempt. Ignore him.

You cross to the podium and begin with a few words. Good evening, gentlemen. Opening the score and announcing the first piece. A Schubert four-part anthem. Schubert was neglected, you tell them, but is a very important composer. You mention the

C Major Symphony, 'The Great', that you yourself rescued from oblivion. Show them how much you know, how much you care.

Why have they started singing already? Why are you conducting so soon? Herr Tausch is in the back row, shaking his head. Perhaps you didn't actually speak your opening address out loud. You meant to...

And their tempo is much too fast. Slow them down. They must be slowed down. Even if it turns into a battle between their voices and your arms marking a safer time. Slowing them, steadying them. Letting the music breathe. Giving each note its right to be heard, to become part of the whole harmony.

They've stopped. They're looking at you. Herr Tausch is saying something.

Two responses: you can slam the score shut, walk out the door and leave them. Or you carry on doing the job you are paid to do.

So, begin again. Back to bar one...

That was the front door closing. Having insisted on bringing you home, Tausch and the others have now left. Clara will soon be coming upstairs to tell you what they said. Their schemes, their insinuations, their hypocrisies.

The phrase of silence at the heart of each person's life – how vulnerable it is to all such noise, such accusations, trivialities and babble. No one knows this better than you. Like the city itself, this silence must be protected. Clara will come shortly. She is preparing what she is going to say, she is trying to find the right words.

With her arms around you and that loving tone of voice breathing its life into you, nothing else matters.

The rest of the city is sleeping. You have got out of bed quietly so as not to disturb her. Tip-toe down the stairs to the cold front room. You sit at your desk, light the candle.

Take out your music manuscript where everything will be laid bare. Your life will be stripped down to those moments of

nty and longing; the burden of human frailty will pass
ie hesitant note to the next. The solo violin reduced to its
tal utterance as, part by part, the other instruments of the
orchestra fall away, leaving it in isolation.

Epilogue

Here you will be cared for; here you will be safe. Some days you
seem to be Florestan, on other days Eusebius; more and more
rarely you appear as Robert Schumann.

Your neighbour in the room next door believes he is a train
running between Dresden and Düsseldorf; Napoleon lives a few
rooms further down, with the Anti Christ on one side and, on the
other, a boiled egg that's not quite ready and never will be. Many,
many lost souls are given sanctuary in this place. The train, you
believe, is the most interesting.

Cheerful and with a purpose in life, the man makes his way up
and down the wards and corridors, calling out stations, taking on
water and passengers. On a good day he regales his fellow inmates
with an ongoing travelogue describing the countryside and cities
he's passing through. Which grants you a refreshing glimpse of
other times, other places. You are lucky that his sense of railway
geography is as poor and disconnected as his sorry mind: Dresden
to Düsseldorf via Paris, Madrid and Macao. Today you are
travelling via San Francisco and the moon.

Jean Sibelius is invited to run away and join the circus

Far, far away, the surface of the black river Tuenola had finally frozen over. It was a windless afternoon. The only sound the creak of ice as it settled deeper, claiming layer upon layer of the chill water; the motionless fir trees lining the banks were no more than stretches of greater darkness in a landscape of failing light.

Sibelius could picture the scene easily – indeed, he had often set it to music. But not for a very long time.

Sitting wrapped in a sheepskin-fleece on the wooden veranda of his house at Järpvenpää where he had lived for more than fifty years, he watched the day collapsing around him. A world-famous composer, ninety-one years old – and his ruthless drive for perfection had stopped all creativity dead. Soon he would be so drunk that nothing mattered.

Neat vodka – not on the rocks, but poured already several degrees below freezing. The first few swallows had tasted of harsh sunlight...and only now did each glass bring the comfort of deepening shadows. His eighth symphony had been written and rewritten over and over again until, after twelve years of self-torment, he had destroyed every sketch and plan, every last cancelled note: page after page of laborious manuscript had been fed to the stove in one final act of renunciation – and release. From then on, silence. The harsh sunlight of hope, the twilight of gathering despair – which was worse?

It had been a quarter of a century since that glorious conflagration, and getting drunk at least led somewhere: to oblivion.

Just then the clowns appeared.

At first Sibelius thought the three red-nosed, banana-footed entertainers had to be an impurity in the homemade spirit. They trooped around the side of the house in a small procession through the snow: the leader in long-tailed evening dress and topper, the second a white-faced pierrot, the third turning cartwheels. Top Hat piped them to a halt on an imaginary flute. They stood in the garden looking directly up at the composer.

'How's tricks?'

Not the DTs then.

A large sip to bring his visitors into better focus.

'You're Sibelius, aren't you?' Top Hat raised his invisible flute and played, quite distinctly, the clarinet solo that opened his first symphony.

'That was a very long time ago,' was the composer's only comment.

'And this?' The final theme from *Tapiola*, his last completed work, published some forty years later.

'Seems even longer.'

'And this?' The clown blew as if across the mouthpiece, letting his fingers caper wildly up and down the stops, but no sound came. He shrugged, then took his imaginary flute in both hands and mimed breaking it in two over his knee.

Sibelius said nothing.

Top Hat smiled up at him: 'That's that done with.'

His companions joined him in a three-man chorus singing, 'Come with us, come with us! Come and join the circus!'

Cartwheel Man did the most glorious spins, a blur that rose into the air till he was spinning around the heads of his companions like a shared halo.

Sibelius looked on, taking sips from his glass every few moments.

The singing came to a halt. Cartwheel Man resumed his feet. The three clowns stared up at him: 'Well then?'

'When I go back indoors – you'll all disappear. Not the woods, the snow, the lakes and the darkening sky. Just you three. As if you'd never been.' Sibelius laughed. 'Which you haven't anyway.' With a great effort he heaved himself up from his seat and turned as if to go, but then faced them again. 'As I'm a well-brought-up old man – before I go I'll have the politeness to bid you all goodbye.' He gave them a wave and again turned towards the house.

'Oh no, you won't!' they chorused.

'Oh yes, I will!' he instantly pantomimed back. Then a moment later asked, 'I won't – what?'

'Won't go back indoors.'

'Just watch me.'

Turning away, Sibelius fixed his eyes on the veranda floor and began his elderly-man shuffle across the wooden balcony: left foot slid six inches forward, pause, right foot dragged up level with it. Left foot slid another six inches forward, then the right. Then another pause.

Inside he could hear the girl from the village. Annukka? Or was that the last one, the one who would dust the telephone and leave it off the hook, sometimes for days? She was getting the evening meal prepared. The stove would be warm; he would put on the wireless; he would sit, drink and wait for dinner.

Left foot forward, and again the right. He must be almost at the door now. Easy does it, easy does it.

'We told you you wouldn't go back indoors!' Top Hat grinned up at him and helped him down the veranda steps. Gently.

How had he ended up here?

'Come with us, come with us! Come and join the circus!' the clowns chorused in a stage whisper, then smiled and took him by the arm.

With every step through the snow Sibelius felt the years falling away. By the time they'd reached the edge of the wood bordering his garden, he had recovered all the vitality of a man in his prime. Fifty years old, say – the age at which he'd completed his Fifth Symphony, that work of total affirmation – with two more symphonies and the tone poem *Tapiola* still to come. Exhaustion and despair lay behind him – ahead, the vigour of a creative life. He had to keep going, striding along with his three companions. So happy did he feel, he considered inviting them to form a train to go *choo-chooing* across the snow at a jog-trot. His breath steamed out in the cold air: 'Are you really from a circus?'

Top Hat doffed his hat. 'Of course.' He pointed to Cartwheel Man, who was curvetting in and out between the trees, making a buzz-saw sound, 'Where else would the likes of us belong, d'you think?'

Sibelius laughed. 'Where else indeed! Especially in this day and age.'

Pierrot cleared his throat. 'I must point out that our circus – the one we belong to, I mean – is a circus for all days and throughout all ages.'

'Our new friend here was just being conversational, that was all,' said Top Hat.

'Granted.' But Pierrot did not look as if he would ever grant anything very much. 'I just wanted everyone to be clear on the matter.' He turned to the composer: 'Saves all sorts of misunderstandings later on.'

Sibelius merely nodded. He'd only been half-listening to Pierrot, being too exhilarated at his recovered vigour and strength. The smell of the wood, the chill freshness of the undisturbed snow, the wind's stillness; his steady tramping on fallen needles, with hardly a sound.

'Is it far?'

'To where?'

'Your circus.'

'No. Never far.' Pierrot was clearly anxious to keep everything exact and proper.

Top Hat halted. 'You want to turn back, maybe?'

Just then the wood began thinning out. They had come to the bank of a river, an empty stretch of water reaching far into the distance.

'It's completely frozen. We can walk across.'

'But where are we —?' began the composer.

No one was listening. Top Hat had produced his flute again and was playing the cor anglais solo from *The Swan of Tuenola*. Like the Pied Piper, he led the others across the ice. Sibelius hurried after.

A mist was rising. Ahead he could hear the line of unbroken melody drawing them into the darkness. A formation of Arctic geese passed overhead. Their honking seemed to fill the sky... and then there was only silence. The clowns had gone.

Sibelius called after them. No reply. He called again. Nothing. The mist was like breath clouding a black mirror, the night. For the first time since leaving his home, he could feel the coldness seeping into him.

Very soon he was shivering, stumbling this way and that, blundering and slipping in all directions. If he'd brought the sheepskin-fleece he might have had a chance. He pictured it lying across his veranda seat, the thick wool with its warmed-oil scent. Back there he had been an old man dying slowly, here he was young and dying rapidly. Some choice! He had been invited, and abandoned.

Then, as if some unseen hand had wiped the night sky with the casualness of Annukka wiping condensation from the kitchen window, the mist cleared. At once, the stars were restored, pinpricks of light across the darkness like so many snapped-off icicles. From far in the distance came the sound of Top Hat's flute tracing out faintly the opening notes of the symphony he had battled with for so long and finally destroyed. The music became louder – trumpets and drums, a full circus band. His eighth symphony, with all its parts miraculously completed!

Soon he was thundering across the ice in a joyful and frantic scramble of sliding and slithering. Surely they were playing his music to welcome him? Deep sustained bass chords overlaid with fragmented woodwind filled the darkness, the whole driven ever onwards by an urgency of strings and brass —

Too late he realised the ice had come to an abrupt stop...with nothing beyond but the emptiness of space. For a split-second he remained poised on the edge. The spread of stars lay everywhere around him – and his unwritten music filled the stillness in between, seeming to hold everything in place.

Annukka knew the old man was dead the moment she saw him sitting there, the empty glass resting on his lap, his sheepskin-fleece lying where it had fallen on the veranda floor. 'He's been dead for the last thirty years,' she remembered someone in the village telling her. 'He doesn't live in that house, he haunts it.'

Not any more, she thought. He was the first dead person Annukka had ever seen. Her hand shook as she reached forward to close his eyes.

Richard Strauss and Pharaoh Amenhotep IV – their dreams

The President of the Reichsmusikkammer was in trouble. His new opera was opening next month in Dresden – and his librettist, Stefan Zweig, was a Jew. Had he seriously hoped that no one would notice?

Strauss stepped out of his official car and paused for a moment in the falling snow. It was powdery. Powdery? – already he could feel himself growing anxious. He stared up at the Berlin townhouse he called home. Some days he could feel its four storeys of solid masonry pressing down on him, slab upon crushing slab. On others it seemed paper-thin and weightless, like an illustration drawn for his autobiography say, a pen-and-ink sketch that could be torn apart in a moment. Impossible, of course. Anyway, his wife Pauline would make sure such things never happened. He could always rely on her.

He went up the front steps and let himself in.

Having closed the street door behind him, he shook the snow from his coat and stared down at the polished wooden floor. Another day replete with the responsibilities of high office and the respect appropriate to his professional standing – but here were the usual three mats waiting for him. Pauline also was waiting.

There was an invisible line beyond the doormats connected, or so it would seem, to an electronic sensor implanted in his wife's scream chords. Twice he had crossed that line without paying due homage to the mats and twice the large front hall had been filled, moments later, with servants eager to see the master of the house being humiliated. 'We thought Frau Strauss had been attacked or a Jew had come to the door,' they'd explained. Lying, of course. They knew quite well what had happened, and he knew that they knew, all of which added to his humiliation.

Three mats. One for wet, one for dry and one extra-bristled for that final, between-the-treads scouring. Powdery snow: the President of the Reichsmusikkammer considered the three mats in turn, trying to work out which he was expected to use.

Pauline's sense of fair play kept her silent while he laboured his way towards a decision. She resisted premature comment. She watched. She waited…until he had committed himself. Then she observed him take a step forward, raise a tentative left foot…

'NEIN! When the shoe makes contact with the mat the resultant pressure will lower the freezing-point, and the snow will melt. So. Powdery snow. The wet mat. The *wet* mat.'

His tentative left foot poised in mid-air, the President of the Reichsmusikkammer hopped across to the wet mat and began wiping.

'Correct. You have had a good day, husband?'

Strauss wiped left, then right, then left again. Nodding meanwhile. 'A good day, yes.' All done, he stepped on to the bristle-mat for the final dry-off.

Their evening together: newspaper, dinner, conversation, wireless …then bed. Strauss lay stretched by Pauline's side listening to the creak of the starched sheets and the steady in-out/in-out of her breathing. Some nights he remained awake for hours. There were few certainties in a professional life spent manoeuvering his way around the lunacies of racial aesthetics, but *sleeplessness*, yes, he could always count on that. Or he could until recently…

Ever since he had been officially informed about the consequences of continued collaboration with Stefan Zweig, the Jew, things had been very different. Insomnia had deserted him. Instead, he had found himself drawn into a world growing more familiar every night, a world utterly unlike the one he knew.

And here it was again. Starting all over: the darkness around him separating into shadows, and the scraps of shadow disintegrating into shade upon shade. Complete dissolution. Nothingness. The transition between two worlds – when, briefly, he alone had to bear the full weight of his human terror. Until everything that was, and all that was not, dissolved...into a brilliance of light, into slashes of blue sky, into openings cut in the stonework, into the reds, vermillions and golds of wall-paintings. The rightful place for his true self. Once more he had become God. A god not yet in heaven, but in his very own sacred palace.

Strauss stepped out on to the balcony, into the searing dryness of the desert. In the distance the Nile shimmered like a flash of cobalt-blue lightning in the heat. And the pyramids, their diminishing perspective a treat to the eye, stretched far into the distance. Yes, after a succession of night visits, this too was beginning to feel like home. For convenience, the pyramids were grouped into dynasties. His own was number eighteen and he was Amenhotep IV, also known as the Sun-God. He remembered it all now.

Over to the left he could see slaves toiling away at his own personal contribution to the family collection. Hauling great slabs of stone across the desert was killing work, and every so often a slave stumbled and fell to his knees. Then he was beaten until he got back on his feet, took hold of a rope and started hauling again for all he was worth. If they dropped dead, they were dragged away. Plenty more to take their place, of course.

A distressing business, pyramids. Watching your very own tomb getting built – some days were better than others, but not this one. His Divine headdress refused to sit just right, his Godly raiment seemed a tad too loose where it should have been tight and a tad too tight where it should have been loose; the Divine footwear pinched. He lingered a couple of minutes longer on the balcony, staring out at the slaves, the overseers, the stones, the palm trees, the sand, the sun, the pyramids. Like yesterday all over again. The permanence of Egyptian civilisation. Ho-hum.

Just then one of the slaves, perhaps desperate for a moment's respite in a life of ceaseless toil, glanced up and caught sight of him. Instantly the man prostrated himself on the sand with a sigh, 'Your Divinity!'

Within seconds, the other slaves — all two hundred and fifty thousand of them — had dropped to their knees, foreheads on the sand, and begun sighing communally. The desert reverberated to their salaam of awe in the revealed face of their Godhead. Though he knew it would only cause trouble later, Strauss stayed where he was, basking in the unquestioning adoration. It did feel rather good.

No sooner had he raised a hand in Divine acknowledgement of this worship, notching the collective sigh up nearly an octave, than a cheerful *ping* from his laptop told him he had an e-mail. It was from the Chief Overseer:

'Please, please, please, Your Divinity, you are urged to remove your Divine presence from the balcony. 250,000 men dropping to their knees and ceasing toil for ten minutes equals two point five million manpower minutes of production lost. An equivalent of nearly five years. We have discussed this before, Your Divinity. We beg you to remember that if you want your pyramid ready for your death - *please keep out of sight.*'

Point taken. He returned indoors and settled down with a good papyrus. It failed to grip, however. The thought that had been plaguing him off and on ever since he'd first discovered he was Amenhotep IV, kept returning: was his life no more than a matter of filling in the time before he died and took to his pyramid? He shrugged and pressed the sun-shaped bell set in the wall. A bit of pampering, he thought, might put him in a better mood.

*The desert reverberated to their salaam of awe
in the revealed face of their Godhead*

*

Gradually the sunlight dimmed, the blue Nile and its cataracts leaked away to become a trickle of water running through the old-fashioned plumbing. Strauss awoke; his bedroom was in darkness. He sensed the heaviness and stiffness of sixty-plus years beginning to repossess his body. He cramped, he creaked, he phlegmed, he farted. He tried to remember his dreams. There was an impression of vastness, of bright colours...All gone, as usual.

Breakfast next. Some coffee, some croissants and a good deal of Pauline. There was to be a parade that afternoon, she announced. Her eyes glittered, catching the light like a pair of imperfectly set precious stones. Agate, possibly. 'The Führer himself will be present,' she added, before leaning across the table. 'He will *speak*.'

Strauss munched his croissant.

'All Berlin will attend. The true Berliners. The men and women of pure Aryan blood. Standing shoulder to shoulder, facing the future. Our future. The Führer says that we will succeed because we *must* succeed. It is our Destiny.'

Strauss munched his second croissant.

Finally the President of the Reichsmusikkammer finished his breakfast and stood up. Pauline came round to his side of the table.

'Close your eyes, my husband.'

Taking a cambric handkerchief from her sleeve, she dusted him down.

'You can open them.'

She straightened his tie. 'Now turn around.'

Lifting his jacket at the back she slid open the panel and inserted the small jewelled key that dangled round her neck. A few brisk turns would empower him for the day ahead. Finally he was ready. A kiss on his cheek.

'Now go and compose.'

*

As he worked, Strauss could hear the *tramp-tramp-tramp* of the Führer's soldiers marching along the pavements four-abreast (he could even make out the half-a-beat skip of the man on the outside who had to half-march in the gutter). From nearby streets came the splintering tinkle and crash of Jewish shop-windows being broken; from here, there and everywhere came the din of accusations, denunciations, pleadings and denials; it was a din that always ended in silence. A silence broken only by the relentless *clickety-click*, *clickety-click* of wheels upon rails, the unannounced trains criss-crossing Europe, running to their unnamed destinations. Sometimes it was the din Strauss found unbearable, sometimes the silence.

As his pen filled in the blanks between staves, making the page black with note-clusters, he'd grow calmer. Almost at peace. But it never lasted. Instead, more and more frequently, he had a vague fancy, a longing that was at once inexplicable and yet familiar, to find a sun-shaped bell to push. He knew the bell would be set in the wall, perhaps discreetly concealed behind draperies. Pressing it, he fancied, would lead to a feeling of pleasure, of glorious release. How strange. He continued filling in the staves.

At 8:30 that evening the black stretch limo came for the President of the Reichsmusikkammer and his wife. Sensibly warmed with schnapps and *wurst*, sensibly wrapped in furs for a long night in the open, they climbed in. For their entertainment, a specially installed video-screen slid open in front of them showing highlights from previous rallies. Searchlights, flags, torches, helmets and marching, marching, marching – all to get them into the rally-mood. There were pamphlets on hygiene and purity.

Pauline read aloud the most soul-enriching passages. She tried to sound like the Führer, and succeeded. Strauss sat back in the leather seat and acknowledged to himself that, truly, the world had gone mad. His world and everyone else's.

Again he felt like reaching over to find a sun-shaped bell to press. There was no discomfort, no inconvenience that wouldn't be relieved by pressing that bell. For every problem there is a bell, somewhere. He chanted this unexpected mantra to himself. It seemed to make sense. *For every problem there is a bell, somewhere. For every problem there is a...*

He was jerked awake by a sudden roar from outside, as of a vast crowd. From the smoothness of the progress they were making through the streets of Berlin – no stopping for traffic lights, pedestrians, other vehicles – he could tell that their limo was now part of a cavalcade. Doubtless, if he glanced out of the window, he would see lines of cheering citizens and waving flags, little children and their little flags. Doubtless...but he no longer looked out of windows.

Pauline told him: the Reich will endure for a thousand years.

Quite spontaneously his hand had reached out and found a sun-shaped bell. He pressed it.

The limo had stopped. The door was opened and Strauss stepped out. It was like every Egyptian night he'd ever dreamed of. Total darkness pinpricked here and there by the usual stars in their usual positions. No moon as yet. The eternal stillness of sand, palm trees and pyramids in all directions. The Nile. In their camp the slaves lay motionless, too exhausted even to turn over; the overseers, granted daylong the right to brutalise anyone within reach, enjoyed the dreamless sleep of the therapeutically purged. Strauss knew this was his chance, but he would have to move quickly.

Had there been a moon, his shadow would have been seen flitting between the giant pillars of the temple. No moon meant no shadow, so Strauss moved swiftly and invisibly through the darkness. Fortunately he knew where the giant pillars were.

He could gauge his progress by feeling the texture of the path changing underfoot. Smooth stone slabs gave way to cobbles, then to broken stones, pebbles and, lastly, sand. Every so often a cry came out of the darkness, a jackal, a riverbird – the gods of the night. Like himself.

Less than an hour later he stood at the base of his own uncompleted pyramid. It loomed high above the rubble littering the ground, left-overs from when the masons had chiselled each separate piece of stone into its final shape, ready to be slotted precisely into its predestined position. He began to climb.

The letter was waiting for him on the breakfast table, next to Pauline's plate. She'd saved him the trouble of opening it, and of reading it.

'Good morning, my husband.'

'Good morning, Pauline.'

'Sleep well?'

'Yes, thank you. Letters?'

'You did not mention you were still writing that opera with that Jew.'

'I was meaning to —'

'Anyway, the Jew has fled. You are safe now.' She held out the letter. 'From now on you will work with a new librettist. Dr Joseph Gregor has been officially approved.'

Strauss pushed aside his morning croissant and got to his feet.

'I — I —' he began. More than anything he wanted to smash his fist on the table, to shout out loud. For several seconds he stood staring down at his wife, at the letter, at the uneaten croissant. His hands were clenched at his sides. Then, he wanted to turn away and weep. These, he knew, would be burning tears. He could feel them just behind his eyes, scalding him even as he stood there, unable to speak.

Pauline came round beside him to lay her hand on his shoulder.

He thought to himself: surely I'll flinch at her touch?

But he didn't.

Then he wondered to himself: perhaps her tenderness might ease my tears, letting them flow at last?

But it didn't.

Nothing happened. Husband and wife remained standing together, in silence.

At last she took the jewelled key from around her neck. Then he relaxed. Fully wound up for the day ahead, he left the room, crossed the hall and entered his study, eager to begin work.

The Royal Palace was in an uproar. The Pharaoh could not be found. The Royal bed had not been slept in; the Godly raiment hung undisturbed in its rack. Ditto the Divine headdress. Every pair of Divine footwear was accounted for.

The Royal track was easy to follow. After the smooth paving and cobbles came to an end, the first Royal footstep was clearly seen upon the sand. The trail led to his unfinished pyramid. As no Royal footstep was seen to lead away from it, the implication was obvious. Finally, the entire retinue of court officials, priests and palace guards was clustered together on the ledge just outside the pyramid entrance. Most uncomfortable for everyone.

A runner was sent to the slaves' camp for torches. The corridor would narrow as it neared the burial chamber and so an order of precedence had to be established. This done, the rescue procession entered the pyramid.

Exhausted after his strenuous night, Strauss had made himself comfortable in his Death-boat. A stone pillow for his head, plenty of leg-room to stretch out in, total darkness for the necessary rest and preparation prior to his journey to the Afterworld, he had soon dozed off.

The sound of voices and footsteps echoing along the passage woke him. He arranged himself into the Death-position. Moments later the burial chamber had filled with the glare of rush-lights, flickering shadows and a reverential silence. The Chief Priest spoke: 'Your Divinity, we are pleased to find you safe.'

Behind him, the line of lesser priests, court officials and warriors all dropped to the floor, most of them being forced to shuffle awkwardly backwards into the corridor again to give themselves room. In chorus they offered thanks for the safety of their Pharaoh.

Amenhotep IV sat up. 'Nothing's changed? Nothing changes.' He gave a gesture of Divine encouragement. 'So carry on with my pyramid. I'll stay here. Build it around me.'

'But – but, Your Divinity —'

A gesture of the Royal hand silenced their protestations.

'Build it good and strong. It's got to last.'

As he heard their footsteps stumbling away down the corridor, he relaxed, easing himself back down to full-stretch. The flickering from the torches became fainter and soon there was complete darkness once more, and complete silence. Here he could dream without the bother of having to keep his eyes shut. Dream of faraway Berlin, dream of Herr Richard Strauss, the President of the Reichsmusikkammer, being wound up for his morning's work, dream of Pauline guiding the composer safely through the terrors of the Third Reich...

He was just settling himself into the Death-pose when he had a thought. Having fumbled in his tunic, he pulled out his mobile. He'd text the Chief Overseer a message to have a sun-shaped bell put in. Doubtless a bit of pampering now and again would help him get through eternity. Would the stone slabs stop the signal? There was only one way to find out. Message completed, he pressed *Send*, then lay back down to wait.

Tchaikovsky decides which world he belongs to

He'd been woken by a *tap-tap-tap* on his bedroom window. A branch moving in the wind, perhaps? Or had he been dreaming? Tchaikovsky sat up and stared ahead into the darkness. Not a sound. Of course not. He was far from the noise and bustle of Moscow. The shooting-lodge, where he was staying, was part of the country estate of his patroness, the Countess Von Meck. He pictured the lake, the fields and woods beyond.

Tap-tap-tap it went again. Not a dream then, but the composer knew he'd never get back to sleep. Time was supposed to speed up as you got older; not for him, though. The last year had sometimes seemed like ten as he'd lain awake in various empty rooms listening to the frantic tick of his pocket-watch on the bedside table. He'd tried everything: drink, drugs, sex and more herbal remedies than he could remember. Nothing worked.

The downstairs clock chimed the half-hour. Exactly which particular half-hour he wasn't sure. Later rather than earlier, he hoped. There were matches and a candle within reach; he leaned towards them, then let his hand drop. Outside a cloud must have drifted across the face of the moon and away again, as faintly, and then more strongly, a wash of metallic light soaked into the room.

He could see now what had woken him: some overgrown ivy scraping against the window-pane.

After taking a sip of water he decided to get up. He was quite alone in the house. The servant had been given the night off and was probably still in town, and probably still drunk. Loneliness Tchaikovsky felt only in crowds, not here. Since the end of his disastrous marriage, he treasured his solitude.

Ten minutes later, having dressed and gone downstairs, he stood at the open front door. How still the night was: not a breath of wind, not a sound. After standing for several moments to let the darkness and calm seep into him and soothe, he crossed the stretch of gravel at the front door and stepped on to the grass. His footsteps now almost soundless, he passed through an archway of roses, across the lawns and down a set of stone steps leading to the parkland. In the distance the small lake lay like scratched silver, like a tear in dark cloth. He began making his way towards it.

All at once, as though a stage technician has thrown the switch for every stage light in the house, the scene around him bursts into brightness. In this glare, the trees seem like scribbles of branches and trunks on pasteboard, the lake a brushstroke, the parkland and countryside beyond just so much painted scenery. An empty stage. The setting for a play. A ballet. Action:

Someone is coming towards him carrying a tray.

As Tchaikovsky's eyes grow accustomed to the light, he can make out people standing all around. Some are chatting, some laughing. There's no one he recognises. Neither Anton Rubinstein, nor Nikolay, nor his own brother Modest. These are all strangers.

'You're tired. You must drink.'

Now that the tray is being presented to him, he can see who's holding it. A young man. A teenager, really. Familiar-looking and rather attractive. But they haven't met before, or have they? He would surely remember. What he wants is to reach out and stroke the side of the young man's face. Not as an invitation, not any more. Simply as an acknowledgement of momentary beauty, of youth; of possibility in an all but impossible world.

Despite the warmth and near-intimacy of their letters, he's never actually met Countess Von Meck. Are these perhaps friends of hers? She knows about his marriage – those nine weeks of madness – his flight and attempted suicide. Standing all night in the freezing waters of the river Neva, for God's sake! Who was the mad one, his crazy wife or his crazy self?

'Drink!'

The young man is holding out the tray, urgency in his eyes. Such a look of concern. Compassion.

'Drink.'

'But won't it kill me?'

And how they all laugh! 'Of course it will!' comes the answer. They laugh and laugh, catching each other's eyes, pushing their faces close to his while making grotesque, conspiratorial winks: 'But you know that already, don't you?'

As he reaches for the glass, the ballet scenery dissolves around him, falling into tatters. Harsh daylight claws its way through. Everywhere he looks, grass and trees crumple up as if too near heat. The sky is being torn open.

Tap-tap-tap. It was night again. Another night, years later. He sat up in bed, his room was flooded with moonlight. The frantic *tick-tick* of his heart. That's what had wakened him, that surge of adrenalin coursing through his body to set his heart hammering against his chest as though it were shaking the bars of the cage holding his life within.

No dream this: the loveless bed, the furniture like different shades of darkness, the window framing the countryside beyond. A sense of absence and emptiness papered over. So much ballet-scenery.

That rush of adrenalin. Yes, he had been dreaming again of the young man serving drinks in the Countess's garden. Another night, another dream. The young man recognised him and invited his affection. But when feelings are a running sore that only a lover's hand can touch, and heal...what remains when that hand, as it must be, is removed?

Tchaikovsky has come to a decision. With his Sixth Symphony completed, he will allow himself a few days more. He has given the world his dreams and his art, and he will finish by giving it everything. His decision will bring lasting peace. Dramas of love and death set to a precise choreography are only a brief release. The rest is a terrifying chaos of the heart.

One last ballet then, with himself as creator, performer, director and audience. It will end as every day has ended: he returns to an empty house, a solitary bed. To dreams he wakes from with his face covered in tears.

He will pretend it is the attractive young man who is offering him the final glass from his tray. His last indulgence.

Tafelmusik and cat-scarers: a brief biography of the real Georg Telemann

Preface

A *glance at the* Hamburg – Our Historic City *handbook shows the unfashionable part of the city where the great composer lived to have been an etching of timber-framed houses huddling together for support while their windows leaned across the narrow streets to gossip with the windows opposite. Taking up most of the sky was an ornamental scroll announcing in Gothic script:* HAMBURG c.1600; *but by Telemann's time the writing would surely have been smeared to near-illegibility after more than a century's rain and Baltic sea-mist.*

It was here that a man whose name was celebrated the length and breadth of Europe, lived and died in utter obscurity. How could this have happened? Only recently, from the notes, receipts and mail-order catalogues that have come to light, has it been possible to piece together the facts of his solitary and dedicated life. The real Telemann was a true artist, not an over-productive crowd-pleaser-cum-virtuoso of sharp business-practice, as the commonplace biographer would have it. The fact is, for the last two hundred and fifty years these academic slipshods have been writing about the wrong man...

A brief biography of the real Georg Telemann

Another day, another hangover.

. The young lawyer was not a happy man. If his second-hand wig depressed him, the view from the window of his empty office depressed him even more. In the absence of any litigation, or any prospect of it, his dining-table/office desk was cluttered with dishes of gherkins, salted herring, a selection of discoloured salami and empty bottles. When the neon-bright pickles started flickering off and on too harshly, he turned away. But not quickly enough...

His contribution to the colourful street life below his window concluded, he breathed in deeply, steadied himself and tried to remember what he'd been composing the previous evening: a new mass, another setting of the Passion, an opera? Who would ever know? More to the point, who cared? His full-time failure as a lawyer was matched only by his after-hours' failure as a composer. By day he wore a wig and sat in an empty office, by night he wrote music that was never played. Some life.

Returning to the table he noticed that while he'd been feeling sorry for himself, his hangover had completed the entire first movement of a concerto for two violins and chamber orchestra. In the key of D minor, which said it all.

Later that morning he took his hangover for a walk to the far side of the Alster and back, and managed to lose it. All at once the sun was shining.

Just then a courier van pulled up beside him.

Telemann was still trying to focus on the van-high Day-Glo lettering: TOMORROW'S MAIL – TODAY! – when he felt a tap on his shoulder.

'Herr Telemann, sign here.' The courier, logo-ed efficiently from peaked cap to toe-cap, was holding out a clipboard.

Where Telemann the unsuccessful lawyer became instantly suspicious, Telemann the unsuccessful composer was at once sadly flattered. He reached for the proffered quill.

'My autograph?'

Day-Glo man gave him a professional smile and a bulky parcel.

In years to come Telemann was to remember the next few moments with moist-eyed affection: it was as if the etching that was the historic Hamburg he knew and loathed down to the last stain on its ornamental scroll, had been suddenly scrunched into a ball and thrown away, forever. In its place – a glorious new city crammed with undreamed-of possibilities.

Not immediately, however. Not until he'd got his legal-sharp teeth on to the job and had managed to tear open the heat-sealed plastic wrapping. What could it be? he wondered.

Then he remembered.

It must have been a month or more since he'd taken his lucky groschen to the charity scratchcard. A vigorous scrape: then one – two – three holiday *schlösser* had appeared in a line. Twenty-five point lettering announced: CONGRATULATIONS! and told him he was the lucky winner of a *schloss* complete with turrets, moat and driveway-drawbridge, or cash up to a trillion groschen. GUARANTEED! All he had to do was tick a few boxes. Could this package be his big prize?

He ripped off the last of the plastic wrapping. Inside, a cheque for one groschen, and a book heavier than ten bibles rolled into one. So, no holiday *schloss*.

He was about to bin the mail-order catalogue into the Alster when a sudden breeze riffled open the pages. He gazed down at the shiny paper, at the illustrations. And he gasped. What a brilliance of colours! What a blaze of new light for the new day dawning around him! He looked, and was hooked!

His face glowing, he flicked through page after page. Strange, unfamiliar emotions stirred deep within him. For the first time in his life he wanted...and wanted...and wanted. He'd no idea what a cordless flymo was – but he wanted one. Maybe even two. He flicked, he saw, he craved. Same for the shelf-units, the vegetable shredder, the reversible dinner-jacket...

Even in his darkest hours he had always believed a day would come when there would be more to his life than a wig, an empty office, a clavichord and round-the-clock failure. Well, here was that day, and here were the glossy pages to prove it! Self-assembly garden-sheds, solar-powered fountains, interlocking rones. Every page a revelation.

The following weeks passed in a blur of ticking boxes, deleting where appropriate, selecting size, colour, style, coding. He rose early and lived each day to the full − no more *bierkeller* and *weinstuben* for him. No more hangovers. He framed his one groschen cheque and hung it above the mantelpiece. Never had he felt more alive. The law was a dud. Time for Plan B.

He was a composer, wasn't he?

And he was living at the high point of the North German Baroque, wasn't he?

North German Baroque pretty much dominated European music − right?

All he needed was good marketing.

So he bombarded court chamberlains, princes' private secretaries, kapellmeisters and concert promoters with cantatas, symphonies, Passions, trio sonatas, concertos. He'd a trunkful of the stuff, after all. He quill-and-inked, he petitioned and pleaded, he knocked on doors, ran after sedan chairs…He networked.

The next few months passed in an even greater blur as the mail-ordered goods started to arrive or, more frequently, failed to arrive. It was six flights down to the street: after the first week the maid refused to answer the door during postal hours, and so did his wife. In his eagerness to get cataloguing, he'd kept no proper record − indeed no record at all − of what he'd ordered. The bell would ring, he'd rush down to find a set of garden furniture, say, and no memory of ever having ordered them. A spontaneous whim, perhaps: once ticked, instantly forgotten.

Soon he was up and down the stairs a dozen times a day to collect extendible wine racks, clocks that chimed a different birdsong for every hour, etc. He embarked on a fierce correspondence with the catalogue company, returning items, querying delivery dates, demanding refunds. He muddled and remuddled his credit balance, changed orders, re-ordered again; forms went astray or crossed in the post. He asked the catalogue company to refer to previous correspondence, to ignore previous correspondence; he sent them registered letters, recorded delivery. He cancelled cheques; he cancelled orders and they arrived anyway, usually wrong.

Almost to the day when the last of his trio sonatas had been returned unplaced to join everything else back in the trunk, his credit ran out. The arithmetic was very straightforward:

No music + no credit = no hope.

He knew the moment of truth had arrived. His destiny stared at him, and he stared back. What was he to do? Give it all up and don the wig once more? Or else rise above the chaos he had created and, as it were, soar on wings of spiritual growth – a wiser and better man?

Telemann did neither.

Buried beneath the next day's correspondence from the catalogue company filling the Telemann letter-box – their usual collection of vicious claims, counter-claims, accusations and denials – was a most attractively printed flyer. To the beleaguered composer it was a flyer from heaven:

WINDOWS CLEANED

DOGS WALKED

MUSIC OF THE NORTH GERMAN BAROQUE AGENTED

Telemann was about to learn the meaning of the phrase 'lifestyle-makeover'.

Seeing how desperate was his client's situation, the newly engaged agent took up residence *chez* Telemann. Moving into the best room and with the best view, he got down to work immediately. He was tireless: power-lunches, cocktail parties, CD promotions, the festival circuit. In less than a fortnight he'd placed several masses, two operas and a complete cycle of church cantatas for every

Sunday of the year. The chamber music made excellent introductory free gifts. Their strategy meetings were brief: he'd simply tap the composer on the chest, smile and say, 'More Passions, more *tafelmusik* – and keep it coming!'

Telemann's wife left him, his children left him. He hardly noticed. Next to go was the maid. Soon every room in the house – the agent's excepted – was stacked with labour-saving devices, novelties, gifts and handy household gadgets. Between writing furious letters to the various catalogue companies he was now signed on with, and composing the required *tafelmusik*, Telemann no longer had time to attend his own concerts. He didn't miss what he'd never had. Also, there were no more hangovers, no more walks around the Alster; the world had become an occasional glance out of the window or a dash to and from the post office. He was a happy man, composing day and night, cataloguing at will.

In an effort to keep up production, he rearranged arias into instrumental movements and vice versa; settings of the Passion were cannibalised into several months' worth of cantatas. He consoled his artistic conscience with a little motto he gothic-scripted for himself and hung next to the one groschen cheque:

A good composer is a good recycler.

His agent was nobody's fool, least of all Telemann's. He started a magazine, *Der Getreue Musikmeister*, which featured his client's latest compositions – a single movement at a time. If the subscribers wished to have the complete work, then they had to keep subscribing. This stroke of business genius swept Europe and raised his client's profile till it towered above those of all other composers bar none. Not that the agent bothered the composer with such details, of course. Rather, realising what a good thing he was on to, the agent did all he could to feed Telemann's catalogue habit. Sometimes he intercepted the postman, substituted wrong items, cancelled others, placed spurious orders in the composer's name. His own motto, which he never committed to any script, gothic or otherwise, was: 'A frantic composer is a productive composer.' He made contracts on Telemann's behalf, attended concerts on his behalf, occasionally conducting and whenever possible taking bows in the composer's name.

Gradually rumour got round that this man himself was, in fact, the real Georg Telemann. (No prizes for guessing who probably started the rumour!) To go among Society as a 'Successful Businessman', rather than 'Music-scribbler', showed a proper willingness to conform to the social decencies and society politely acceded to this harmless deceit. Indeed, Georg Philipp Telemann, as the agent soon came to be called, was welcomed and lauded wherever he went.

Meanwhile, back in the attic room he had moved into due to increasing lack of storage space, the real Telemann was profoundly grateful. Being a true artist he wanted only to be left alone to devote himself to his art. And to the latest catalogue. After the distress of his early years, he had reached a refuge of emotional and creative balance. Happiness, of a sort. And this modest biographer wishes he could close his brief study with that heart-warming picture. But life is not like that, nor is art…

Epilogue

Many years passed. One evening the agent – whom we shall now call Telemann, as everyone else did – came home for a quick shower before heading out to an awards ceremony. Also, he wanted to see if there was anything new since lunchtime that could be unloaded on to the open market.

As he climbed the narrow stairs to the composer's attic room, he admired the satisfying click his dress shoes made on the uncarpeted steps. He paused outside the door before knocking, surprised not to hear the customary rustle of catalogue items being unwrapped, the scratch of quill on parchment, or else gentle snoring. Tonight there was only ominous silence.

The agent knocked. And waited.

Knocked again.

Went in.

The first thing that registered was a new manuscript on the keyboard. He picked it up and hummed through a few bars. Yet another violin concerto, but it sounded OK. He had just started rolling it up when, from across the room, there came a heartfelt groan of despair.

He looked over to see the aged composer at his desk surrounded by the usual litter of jiffy bags, bubble-wrap, polystyrene filler, order forms, return forms, current and past catalogues. He was holding something to his ear, shaking it, and holding it up again.

'Twenty-seven times I've returned this to them...and it still doesn't light up!' He gave the sagging piece of plastic a final shake-and-listen, then very carefully replaced it on his desk. There was a lifetime's sadness in the gesture, sadness and regret.

'A cat-scarer, that's all. Supposed to be inflatable, luminous and ultra-sonic. Battery-operated.'

After a long pause he glanced towards the agent and for the first time in years looked him straight in the eye. 'Well, I suppose that's that,' he sighed. '*Tafelmusik* and cat-scarers. Can you tell me what it's all been about?'

The two men stared at each other in silence. After several moments the old composer got to his feet, slowly and laboriously. He seemed exhausted. He made his way over to his bed, and lay down.

'What has it all been about?' he whispered to himself. Without another word he turned to face the wall.

Agent Telemann remained where he was, as if pondering the composer's question. Possibly he was deeply moved, possibly not.

When he left shortly afterwards, he took the new concerto with him. It had sounded like all the others, which meant it would sell like all the others...and that was good enough for him.

He was holding something to his ear, shaking it

The Mighty Handful versus the rest of the world

Had the five Russian composers who made up The Mighty Handful been less stubborn, they could have been playing indoors – indeed, one of the ballrooms of the Winter Palace had already been placed at their disposal. They were offered Brussels lace coverlets for goal-netting, extra chandeliers for floodlighting and wigged servants for corner flags. Such a luxurious all-weather pitch, with every facility, would have cost them only a couple of waltzes each, but they'd refused.

'We're nationalist composers,' piped up Cui. 'We don't *do* waltzes.'

Rimsky-Korsakov – who was to orchestral colouring what a chameleon is to tropical undergrowth – suggested a compromise set of Polish-style mazurkas.

'*Waltzes*,' the Court Chamberlain insisted. 'Strauss-style.'

The rest is history. Throughout the winter season The Mighty Handful were forced to play their five-a-side home games in a local park where, from October onwards, the snow fell thickly, and daily. Blizzards were frequent.

*

Today was a grudge match. As they got themselves into the shorts and boots under the protective canopy of umbrellas held by liberated serfs, *muzhiks* and the team's *droshky* driver, the talk had been defiant.

'See these Rubinstein brothers and their Conservatory team! A bunch of — shit!' Mussorgsky was so wound up he'd snapped a lace. 'The pair of them trying to play a European game. Well, they're not Europeans —'

'Neither are we!' Balakirev interrupted, 'We're Russians!!'

'RUSSIANS!' Cui stood to attention and saluted.

'That's the right spirit.' Professor Borodin glanced over and smiled an indulgent, professorial smile at the plucky composer who'd only just managed to make The Mighty Handful team on the strength of a polka and variations for piano. The older man stopped himself just in time from reaching across to give the recent signing — whose name he could never remember — a professorial pat on the head. 'Everybody ready?'

The Five got to their feet for the pre-match photo-call. As winter deepened, this part of the fixture took up more and more time. The wind came from the north-east across the Siberian plains driving the snow before it, so the serfs, *muzhiks* and the *droshky* driver were re-grouped into a line to shield the composer-players from the blizzard long enough for Sergei Sergeivitch to take the team photo.

Sergei Sergeivitch hadn't asked to be the team photographer, and didn't want to be. If the truth were told, he didn't want to be a photographer, period. Having grown up in the village of N— in the province of K—, he had come to St Petersburg determined to become a Russian novelist. His own small village boasted few Russian novelists, but the city, he soon discovered, was stricken with them. And a gloomy crowd they were. At nights they gathered on the Nevsky Prospect to draw lots for the best lamp-posts to hang from or formed a queue to jump into the frozen Neva — declaring the vast and unendurable emptiness of the Russian Steppes to be a metaphor for the yearnings of the Russian soul.

They talked a lot about soul. In less than a fortnight Sergei Sergeivitch had switched to photography.

Why photography? people asked.

Well, why not? – was his reply. Soon he was attending Czar christenings, hunger marches and, like today, snapping football teams.

'Smile, please!'

As always when being photographed, Mussorgsky stared at the hooded figure and felt himself growing tense all over. Recently, against a team of Young Nihilists, he'd let in four sitters, including a between-the-legs nutmeg. He was hard at work on his opera *Boris Godunov* – heavy going even when he hit mid-season form – and the resultant crisis of self-doubt had cost him a week's work. Some days it felt *Boris* would never be finished. Which made it difficult to smile on command. He bared his teeth.

Pouf! The magnesium flare lit up the huddle of players, their ice-stiffened beards and chilled knees. One more for burial at the bottom of the inside back page, thought Balakirev, who despaired of his club ever receiving the write-ups it deserved. The Rubinstein brothers, academic lickspittles unable to tell the top of a ball from the bottom, were now fielding a team that included three ex-pats from the German Late Romantic Movement – free transfers if he ever saw them. These reactionary throwbacks got more coverage than they knew what to do with: their training sessions and concert rehearsals got full-page spreads, their team photos were centrefolds. Last Sunday, Anton Rubinstein's most recent piano concerto, a sepulchrally mock-Teutonic effort in D Minor, had been puffed in all the supplements with accompanying league tables detailing the team's form and cup chances.

'Connections!' Balakirev spat the word into the snow, and watched it freeze.

The snowstorm was getting worse. Every so often the ball came hurtling out of the blizzard – sometimes Mussorgsky was ready, sometimes he wasn't. He had been booked for talking to himself.

Pouf! The magnesium flare lit up the huddle of players, their ice-stiffened beards and chilled knees

'Speech patterns,' he had protested as the yellow card was hoisted to invisibility in the storm, 'I'm basing the libretto on speech patterns and need to run through them for —'

The referee was having none of it. A yellow card it was. One more booking and he'd be on the bench. They were trailing six down already...

Later, on the team *droshky* home, the same thought – *Couldn't we drop Cui and sign up Tchaikovsky?* – was on everyone's mind. On everyone's mind but Cui's, of course. But they were The Mighty Handful: five nationalist composers determined to put Russia on the map. The flyers had been printed, there was a wagon-load of T-shirts, scarves, mugs, souvenir strips. Like it or not, till the team merchandise was shifted, they were stuck with Cui.

Something had to be done. Something serious.

They got in a firm of consultants.

After this, things naturally went from bad to worse. Against the Bakunin Anarchist Cell Five – who, of course, could field only three players at a time – they lost 15–0.

The consultants were sacked.

To everyone's surprise it was young Cui who came up with a plan. Just in time, too – all the merchandise had been sold bar a few scuffed-looking videos they couldn't even give away.

It was late February. The game, against an Old Believers Select, was scheduled for that afternoon. Balakirev had organised a pre-match team-building session but had been the only one to turn up. Yet again Mussorgsky had pleaded *Boris Godunov* (people were beginning to wonder if the opera existed at all, and wasn't just a life-excuse), Rimsky was working his way through a re-orchestration of the entire back catalogue of Russian music, Borodin was in his laboratory...and Cui?

Well, that morning Cui had woken with a great idea. He knew he was under pressure. Every pretentious match commentator had begun making the same joke: 'Cui – *qui*?'

'I'll show them who!' he'd boasted to his shaving-mirror. 'I'll show them!'

He arrived late, and panting. Straight into the boots, shorts and strip. Ready for the team photo. Being, musically, the lightweight of the group he always felt like the team mascot. But not anymore. Today he was going to be the team saviour.

It started snowing.

Pouf! Photograph over, everyone began running on the spot, flapping their arms. Mussorgsky passed round the bucket of vodka and they were ready.

Considering his junior-league status, Cui drank deep, and he emerged from the team bucket a sombre man. He told the other four to form a huddle. Then, having glanced round to check he wouldn't be overheard, he crouched down to join them.

In a spirit-scorched voice he whispered the mysterious words: 'Real Madrid, 1959.' Then paused.

Only once they realised he'd actually finished speaking, did their four questioning grunts grunt together as one: '...????'

'Real Madrid,' he repeated, then let them into the secret that would one day transform the entire dynamics of international football: 'No more big-toeing it up the park and running after – we'll *pass* the ball to each other.'

'Pass?' they echoed in close harmony.

'Let me explain.' Reaching under his strip, Cui took out the video, *Historic Moments in World Football*. He opened the accompanying booklet and showed his huddled team-mates a series of black-and-white illustrations. Fortunately, these grainy photographs came complete with colourful overlays, computer-simulated dotted arrows and lines, demonstrating the revolutionary approach pioneered by Puskas, Di Stefano and Santa Maria, which was to secure the European Cup for Real Madrid three years in a row.

'...!!!!' came their ecstatic response.

*

The falling snow turned into a snowstorm.

Thanks to Cui's innovative approach that was to be the last time The Mighty Handful ever played together as a team. Previously, their record defeat was 17–0, now it became 27–0. The boots were hung up, the strips torn up for cleaning rags, the remaining merchandise disposed of under the cover of darkness. Balakirev became a clerk in the railways; Borodin decided to stick to chemistry with music as a side-line; Mussorgsky gave himself to *Boris Godunov* and vodka. Rimsky-Korsakov began orchestrating everything he could lay his hands on: overtures, symphonies, tone poems, shopping lists...

Cui they left at the bus stop – with three hours' worth of video tape draped around his neck like so much plastic creeper. The snowstorm got worse. Everything around him, the cobbled street, the pavement, the bus shelter, became more indistinct. Gradually he too was all but erased from sight.

Half an hour later, Sergei Sergeivitch happened to pass by in his pony and trap. Days like this made him regret having given up his career as a Russian novelist and put him right in the mood for a night on the Nevsky Prospect. As he drew level to what looked like a snowbound post-box standing next to a long-abandoned bus stop, he had a sudden inspiration. Surely here was his way forward. He took out his camera.

Pouf! Forget the rewards of artistic compromise, he'd become the very first Russian Conceptualist. *Pouf!* and *Pouf!* again. This pair of *objets trouvés* he'd call: NOTHING TO SAY AND NOWHERE TO GO. A double metaphor for the eternal yearnings of the Russian soul. Perfect.

Having turned into a snow-covered block of ice, and with his mouth frozen half open, Cui hardly noticed the magnesium flashes. He listened to the jingle of the pony and trap grow fainter, then fade to nothing. Afterwards he listened to the silence of the falling snow. No bus was going to come. Ever. But what depressed him most was the injustice of it all: he had bought a return ticket.

From the Russian fairy-stories his mother used to read him he remembered that no one should ever give up hope. Well, he'd try his best not to. Though it seemed he was becoming more of a snowdrift by the second, there was at least one consolation: he was growing so *deliciously* sleepy. Maybe things would look a little better after he'd had a short nap…?

The letters

How Composer Q chose a better life

After a four years' silence filled with honorary degrees, masterclasses, retrospective festivals and CD box-sets of his selected works, Composer Q sat down at the piano one evening, and wept.

Several heartfelt sobs later he heard his e-mail give its cheerful *ping*. He crossed to the computer. A university in one of those countries so often mentioned on the television news. Because of war? Famine? Natural disaster? It was an invitation to...

He stopped reading and pressed *Delete*. He could picture it already: the lost days, the lost luggage, the faces searching his own, the hands reaching to take hold of him as if some of his creativity might rub off, like good luck from a coalman.

He had only recently turned fifty, but it felt like sixty going on eighty. If he were a twenty-four-hour clock, the electronic numbers would be showing 23:50, long past his bedtime.

Before, when the world hadn't cared, he had composed day and night to get its attention. More recently, it had recognised and embraced him – and, over what he regarded as his best years, it had been gradually crushing the life out of him.

These days there was almost nothing left, except:

The honorary degrees, the masterclasses, the retrospective festivals.

And the silence.

An hour passed, then from outside his study window came the whine of a police-car's siren. Directly opposite his house it peaked and dopplered off at full speed through the darkness, its blue light whirling as it headed down the street towards other, busier, lives.

A few second's later the doorbell chimed.

Remembering that his wife was out at a meeting of the Composers' Wives' Support Group, he got up from his chair and went to the front door. En route he checked in the hall mirror for signs of any lingering redness around the eyes. The chimes rang out again. Someone was being very persistent − to offer him a better life, a better gas bill.

'Yes?'

While inspecting for tears he had removed his glasses, and forgotten to put them back on. He peered at the out-of-focus blur shimmering on his doorstep. Man, or woman? Business suit, or boiler suit? Leather jump-suit?

The figure shimmered closer: 'Composer Q?'

'Yes?'

'My name is . . .' Another siren went dopplering past to join in the pursuit.

'Pardon? I didn't quite catch —'

A sudden gust of wind set the newly planted selection of porch-and-patio greenery − from the Marchmont Garden Centre − thrashing the darkness. Rain began to fall.

'Perhaps you'd better come in.' Composer Q stepped back.

His visitor smiled.

'Most kind of you. It's turning rather nasty out here.'

Composer Q closed the door and retrieved his glasses from the hall table.

For the first time he saw his visitor clearly. Man, mid-thirties, smooth-faced, average height, dark hair, dark jacket. Dark muddy shoes. Very muddy. Composer Q knew he should draw attention to the doormat.

'I'm sorry, I didn't catch your name.'

'Sinclair. You won't know me, but —' the visitor gave another smile, 'I know you.'

There was a pause. Composer Q suggested they go through to the lounge. With a bit of luck he'd get the man dealt with and out the door in time to clean up the muddy footprints before his wife got back. Made the place look like a farmyard, she'd say.

His visitor gave the lightest of laughs: 'I hope I'm not interrupting one of the great moments in the history of Western music?'

'No, I was…' Composer Q left the sentence unfinished.

As if to cover any embarrassment, Sinclair remarked, 'Just so.' Then he paused and looked directly into Composer Q's eyes: 'Which is why I'm here. I believe I can help you.'

The visit seemed to have lasted hours but the hall clock was only just striking nine when Composer Q returned to the sitting-room. He opened the patio doors and the kitchen window for a good scour-through draught to clear the air. For several moments he stood in the patio doorway watching the rain bounce off the decorated flagstones and the wrought-iron furniture – it seemed to hiss back at him, before gushing and bubbling down the drain.

'Francis!'

His wife had returned early! He started towards the front hall trying to scuff away the worst of the mud as he went. She was staring down at the carpet. He took a deep breath, bracing himself for the onslaught…and waited.

To his surprise she looked at him and smiled. Then she shook her head indulgently: 'You poor man! Went out and got yourself soaked through! Never mind, I'll soon have the place clean again!'

That was when he remembered the sub-clause (Domestic Relations) Sinclair had suggested they tack on. 'Look on it as this week's Introductory Free Gift. Customer Care, let's say.'

Nice one.

Next day he rose at dawn. A perfect morning, like a full-colour illustration for the Marchmont Garden Centre Summer Catalogue: an impossibly blue sky, dew glistening on the immaculate lawn, a robin on one fence, a blackbird on the other, thrushes and chaffinches in the trees; the garden furniture had never seemed newer, sturdier and more emphatically rust-free. Only 6:30 a.m., but Composer Q was already sketching out the opening bars of a chamber symphony. His first new work in years.

'Some tea, dear?'

He gave a start, then immediately relaxed. Ah, the pleasures of having an upgraded wife. After she'd dealt with the mud the previous evening, she'd served them both a late evening snack of *pflümli* and fellatio. Now here she was at six-thirty, dressed and serving him early morning tea. Composer Q looked up from staves bristling with daring harmonies, rhythmic subtleties and emotional intensities (he could already imagine the rave reviews) and smiled.

'Love some. Thanks.'

Bless Sinclair, he said to himself, a moment later wondering if that was some kind of blasphemy. Not that it mattered. Now that his creativity had returned, nothing else mattered in the slightest.

The perfect weather continued without pause. Blue skies by day, Mediterranean warmth and starry stillness by night. The lawn remained at perfect trim and never needed cutting; no wasps, no weeds; roses in perpetual bloom. The wine bottle refilled and recorked itself each evening, the bread never ran out, the milk never turned. His wife's hair grew longer and darker, her skirts shorter and tighter. When he complimented her she'd smile coyly, saying, 'It must be love.' Then she'd bring out the *pflümli*.

After years of barren silence the music was simply pouring out of him: a string quintet, a song cycle, two symphonies, several piano sonatas. A production line equal to Schubert's. Maybe Schubert, too, had had a visit from Sinclair?

Sinclair's follow-up visit came exactly seven weeks later. 'Just to see how the contract's doing.'

'Doing?' Composer Q hesitated. 'I don't understand.'

'Have you looked at it recently?'

He looked at the contract as little as possible, which meant never.

'No? Well, maybe you should.'

Sinclair shimmered briefly, and was gone.

Immediately he was alone, Composer Q crossed to the bureau, wrenched out the bottom drawer and upended it. Several years' worth of unfiled invoices, receipts and letters cascaded over the carpet. There seemed to be a glow coming from within the heap, giving a muted luminescence to the pile of drab-coloured paperwork. He grabbed the envelope in question. The seal was still unbroken. He tore it open.

As before, it contained a single sheet of parchment, but now – and he could hardly believe his eyes – the parchment was completely blank. No contract, no signature. Nothing. Composer Q turned it over, also blank. He held it up to the light. There was a watermark: a cloven hoof.

He laughed out loud.

'You called me?' Sinclair had shimmered back into substantiality.

'It's completely blank!'

'And…?'

'Well then, there's no contract.'

'I suppose not.'

'I – I don't understand. Does that mean I'm free?'

'If you wish.' Sinclair gave a modest shrug. 'Despite all the dreadful tales they tell about me, I've never yet damned anyone against their will.'

'But who on earth would want that?'

'On earth? Hmm, you'd be surprised.'

'Well, you can count me out.'

'So you'd like everything to be just as it was then? Back to normal life?'

'Yes, yes.' Composer Q hesitated. 'And my work?'

'Oh, you and your work!' Sinclair laughed and wagged his finger. 'Trying to catch me out, were you?' He sighed, 'OK, don't say I'm not generous. You can carry on composing — no strings attached! My parting gift.'

'You're — you're really rather…kind.'

'Yes,' Sinclair shook his head sorrowfully, 'and so misunderstood.'

'Well…thanks.'

'My pleasure.'

The two men faced each other across the sitting-room. There was a brief trembling in the air, and then Composer Q was alone once more.

It was several moments before he realised that he'd started to shiver. Next, his mouth tasted of sickness, his hands were trembling. He looked at them in horror: near-skeletal, like two bundles of broken twigs. Every joint ached, his clothes hung on him. The room had grown suddenly darker, and ice-cold. A chilling wind came gusting in, rain poured down from cracks in the ceiling. There was a stench of mould and decay. Through gaps in the rotted carpet slithered worms, slugs, snakes, snails and spiders. A tightness that had begun clenching his chest was now clutching at his heart, and a slow and relentless *stab-stab* of pure agony hacked at his liver.

Lightning started to flash every few seconds, then every second, then every split-second. As if the celestial wiring for his house, his garden and the world beyond had suddenly gone faulty, the scene around him was rapidly switched on, then switched off; on, then off; on, then off. Daylight/darkness;

daylight/darkness; daylight/darkness...Using the last of his strength, Composer Q dragged himself across to his chair, and there he collapsed.

He sat up retching with exhaustion.

Sinclair returned. 'You called?'

'What —? What's happening? What's this?' The composer's voice was a croak, a dry rasping of breath.

'You wanted things to be normal again? Well, they are.'

'This...isn't normal...good health...nice house.'

'Quite. But that was a very long time ago.'

His chest felt hollow, he struggled to breathe in air and to push out words: 'A...few...weeks!'

'Everything was perfect, wasn't it? Just the way you wanted it. Glorious weather, furious creativity, biddable wife. Everything.'

'Yes...Yes.'

'It took time, though, but I protected you. You don't really think you wrote all that music in a few weeks, do you? Now you're on your own again, you're catching up on *lost* time, as it were.' He gestured to the garden where the abrupt flashes of light and darkness had now steadied to an ever-accelerating blur of days and nights. 'You and that poor body of yours with its untreated ulcers, cancers, running sores...'

'What...do you...want?'

'Oh, but it's what *you* want, Composer Q.' Sinclair smiled, 'That's all that matters.'

'Don't...want this...'

'I'm not surprised – who would?'

A gnawing pain had begun in Composer Q's kidneys, as if he were being eaten from the inside. He gasped in sudden agony.

'Yes.' Sinclair's voice was smooth and comforting. 'You're quite safe now. No worries, eh!' A final smile. 'Goodbye!' Already he was fading from sight.

Composer Q grasped the chair arm and tried to haul himself up. But failed. He fell back into his seat, raised a shaking hand.

'Wait! Wait!'

'You called?' Sinclair materialised sufficiently to catch whatever Composer Q might have to say.

Evening sunlight fills the patio. There is the scent of roses and honeysuckle, the trill of birdsong. A tray of gin, tonic, ice, glasses, cut lemon and a dish of Sainsbury's Seafood Selection plus assorted nuts is set within arm's reach. From through the open kitchen window come the sounds of his wife preparing their meal.

Sometimes things are unbearable: when Composer Q's every waking moment is filled with the grinding of metal-upon-metal as the hall clock's clumsy mechanism gathers itself to toll nine o'clock. These are the bad days, when the final stroke never sounds.

On really bad days the hour he has waited for has already struck — and only the terror of his mortality remains. There is nothing else.

Today, however, is a good day.

'Carol?' he calls.

'Yes, dear. Dinner's nearly ready.'

He sighs with contentment.

Today he has managed to shut out the dreadful whirring of the clock's cogs, spindles and ratchets. He sits sipping the gin that tastes of gin, having been at work since early morning on a score he believes will be his masterpiece. If he works hard enough, he will manage to shut out everything. Then he will bring another perfect day to its close by serving his wife a perfect G&T from the drinks trolley that never empties, under the blue sky of a summer that never ends.

Girls, glamour and real estate: the secret life of Composer X

Love music, outer-space music and music-to-murder-by. Whatever they've asked for — I've written. Whatever I've asked for, they've paid. I have the right homes in the right places and a swimming-pool in every garden. If a divorce costs me a house, I buy two more for next time round, and stay ahead of the game. Cut my life where you will, it's a stick of rock that spells SUCCESS all the way through.

Everyone assumes I am unhappy. Of course they do. It comforts them to believe that someone who has everything really has nothing, and that behind my electronic security gates there beats a broken heart. Composer X's musical genius, they say, has been bartered for baubles and tinsel, for girls, glamour and real estate...

Composer X stared at what he had just tapped out on the keyboard and then erased the last sentence, keeping only the phrase, 'girls, glamour and real estate'. He whispered the words aloud to himself, highlighted them, clicked 'copy' and pasted them over and over, filling up the rest of the screen. And why not? It was true.

Finding himself between marriages recently, he had said 'Yes' to an invitation to write his life story. The publisher's cheque had zeroes ballooning out of the box like so many thought-bubbles. Today he was making a start on Chapter One.

Just then his secretary came in with the mail:

Fan-mail
Hate-mail
Business
Personal
Begging letters
Ex-wives

She placed the six piles on his desk without a word, and left. He hadn't looked at her. That was the agreement. He had three secretaries: one here in Edinburgh, one in New York and one in LA. He knew which was which by the view out the window. Thanks to e-mail, he didn't really need to be in LA or New York or Edinburgh – but he had to be somewhere. And wives needed to shop. All he needed was to work, and that was all he wanted. If he got what he wanted, he was happy – right?

Once written, his music ceased to move him, though it had cinema audiences across the world weeping, raging or trembling for the required number of frames. But the process of creating it, giving it form and emotion-content and, most of all, getting it *just so* – that was what mattered. He didn't care what happened to it afterwards. Probably God felt much the same about the world.

Being between wives made him feel edgy. Best to keep working. Starting with a glance through the morning's correspondence…

Hate-mail first.

This was his favourite, what he thought of as his chilli pepper start to the day. It set his nerves tingling, toned up his muscles and generally got him firing on all cylinders. His hate-mail was usually straightforward venom unencumbered by explanation or punctuation. Accusations of ripping off everyone from Palestrina to Penderecki, including the poison-pen pusher himself, whose work, of course, no one had ever heard a note of; plus insinuations of sexual deviancy and the like. There was never a return address. It was rarely more than a wish-list of abuse along the lines of 'see you Composer X you shit you bum-wipe...' and so on for page after smeary page.

Today's first effort, indecipherable postmark and dated the previous week, was articulate and extremely well argued. The writer sounded genuinely sympathetic, particularly when touching upon Composer X's lack of divine grace and the likelihood that he would probably burn in hell. As if to reinforce its message, the anonymous missive had been neatly lasered on to the paper. Its tone was Wee Free Presbyterian. Composer X had been to the north of Scotland only once and had tried his best to like it. The horizontal sleet lashing the treeless bogland had lashed him too; the people he'd met had been kindly enough in a morose sort of way, greeting him with the reserve one might accord a fellow-sufferer in Hell...

He had hardly finished reading when, out of the corner of his eye, he noticed something was being scrawled across the sky. He got to his feet, went over to the window and squinted up at the red capital letters:

'DID YOU GET MY NOTE, YOU SINNING BASTARD?'

Composer X's first thought was: such public announcements cannot be taken personally, can they? That's paranoia.

At this, and as though someone had adjusted an invisible gas-knob, the letters flamed up with accusation. Moreover, it would be difficult to deny that the fiery arrow was pointing directly at *him*. Envy he was used to – indeed it was nourishment of a sort – but this sort of thing was upsetting. Better to move to a room with a different view, skip the rest of his correspondence and his life story. Best to get straight down to work.

The current project starred an actress who, from the very first rushes, had appeared vaguely familiar. In the past he'd fallen in love with several women with similar skin-tone, hair colour and range of expression. Being currently available to fall in love, he would do so – with her. Love always felt good. She would be his inspiration. Whether she was emerging from the crashed private jet in the opening sequence, or taking part in the warehouse shoot-out, or was staring enigmatically out across a darkened city before breaking down in tears as the credits began to roll – he'd give her the works.

He booted up his work-in-progress laptop and began.

At 12:15 his secretary came in. Lunch.

He sat out on the veranda, and was pleased to note that the letters of fire had vanished. Once more the Edinburgh sky was a depthless summer blue. The morning's work had gone well and he was in love again. What more could a man ask for? He was just eating up the last of his tiger prawns when he saw embossed red letters at the bottom of his plate:

'JOHN KNOX RULES, OK.'

He stared at them, he rubbed at them – but they wouldn't go away.

Five minutes later, he noticed his white wine was rapidly warming up and starting to fizz, froth and bubble. A moment later, the glass became too hot to hold, and he dropped it. The Waterford crystal smashed on the tiles.

Then, right before his eyes, the glass fragments reformed themselves to lie glittering in the sunlight. Their message:

'KNOX AND CALVIN, OK?'

Thirty minutes later, laptop in its carry-case, travelling bag at his feet, Composer X was standing at the front door waiting for the taxi that would take him to Edinburgh Airport. A direct flight to Tenerife, then a local taxi to his house-and-pool at Los Gigantes. He told himself work was going well. He told himself he was in love. He told himself he would survive.

The Agnus Dei of Schubert's Mass in E flat was just beginning when he had to unplug himself and switch it off for landing. Those baleful discords never failed to thrill and lift the spirits. His plane touched down. Within minutes he'd passed from plane to conveyor belt, to baggage reclaim, customs and taxi. Less than an hour later he was letting himself into his *casa*. Darkness had fallen. The security lights came on. An arc of water splashed on to the small illuminated fountain in the paved courtyard, surging up to welcome him.

Indoors, to give continuity to his interrupted day, he put on the Agnus Dei again. Speakers placed throughout the house ensured that Schubert was already there to greet him when he entered each room. Forewarned, the maid service had put milk, bread and fresh fruit into the fridge. The freezer was always kept well stocked. Tired but relieved to be far from Scottish persecution, Composer X stood for several minutes in his garden, breathing in the scents of magnolia and bougainvillea carried on the warm night air. He sighed with pleasure as he listened to the reassuring sweep of waves breaking on the lava-black beach below. Yes, it had been right to come. Tomorrow, after a good night's rest lulled by the sea's ebb and flow rocking him to sleep, he would resume work. He would fall deeper in love. He would be even happier.

The closing chords of the Agnus Dei were fading into the empty night, but he had taken the precaution to stack the CD player so it would be succeeded, seamlessly, by some Scarlatti. Just before he turned to go back inside he raised his eyes for a glimpse of those familiar stars whose silent presence comforts us in our loneliness on Earth.

For several seconds he couldn't move. Where was Orion? The Plough? Where was The Great Bear? He scanned the darkness left to right, top to bottom, diagonally and anti-clockwise. It made no difference. Stars, constellations and galaxies had been swept aside and their brightness re-set across the emptiness of the night sky. The heavens were filled with a vast and glittering text. Unfortunately, it was in Spanish.

Just then the maid rushed in through the main gate. She was carrying a supermarket bag.

'Bottled water, Señor Composer X. I forget. So sorry.'

'Thank you.' He took the bag from her, then cleared his throat: 'Raquel, the stars...ahem...seem very bright tonight. Don't you think?'

Raquel, knowing that the señor was once again between wives, took a couple of steps backwards as if for a clearer view. She glanced up, and caught her breath in surprise. '*Madre de Dios*!'

'And, Raquel, they seem…I mean…different.'

She nodded, 'Si, señor.' She looked deeply shocked.

'Like…like they're trying to tell us something.'

She continued backing away from him. '*Claro*. Is message. Is very terrible.'

'Yes, Raquel, but what does it…? Ahem…Who do you think it is for?'

She was almost at the gate now. She shrugged. Then without looking at him, called out: 'Not me. This I know. I go now.' And she vanished.

Alone again, Composer X wanted to shrug his shoulders and turn away as Raquel had done. He wanted to walk the short distance into his house, to close the door behind him, and lock it.

He stood staring up at the incomprehensible Spanish. When he tried saying the words out loud, they still sounded incomprehensible – and extremely threatening. Like a curse.

Work, he told himself. Love, he told himself.

He went indoors and was soon seated at his laptop: *My darling*, he typed, *you will be my inspiration*…

Twenty minutes later he had finished his heartfelt declaration. He read it through, spell-checked it, then sent it off.

How recent, irreversible changes in the world have affected the life of Composer Y

Remember the time when Y was a little-known composer? Coming between the celebrated X and the no less renowned Z, he knew from early on that things were not going to be easy. And it wasn't just the layout of the alphabet that ensured he had a hard time of it — deciding to make the double-bass his instrument-of-choice was scarcely helpful. With tragic defiance he would address his shaving-mirror every morning: *If Dragonetti can become a household name, then so can I.*

That, of course, was back in the days when everyone struggled to keep up to speed with the best deals in loyalty cards and cashback discounts, with their pin numbers and passwords. While 24,000 people died of malnutrition and 140 species perished daily, the lucky ones among us, at the rate of several a week, became millionaires. Composer Y looked on at this clamour of activity and whenever he felt particularly left out, consoled himself with the deep rich tones of his double-bass.

*

One day, he went for a walk downtown and a good long think about his future. He had just rounded the corner into Princes Street and was wondering whether a concession to popular taste, in the form of a duo for double-bass and Alpine horn, might not raise his market-profile, when he heard his name being called.

He turned, but could see no one. Only the usual: the kilted doorman outside the Balmoral Hotel, the travellers hurrying down the steps to Waverley Station, an orderly bus queue. Had he been dreaming?

As casually as he could, he glanced round in a complete circle – but beyond the surge of frantic go-getters, the instant millionaires and beggars, there was nothing. Just then a maroon Lothian Transport bus pulled up. The assembled queue filed neatly on, flourishing the strips of their Saver Day-Tickets like carnival streamers. Clearly his confusion had gone unnoticed. He continued walking.

The sun was shining and the day just right for some positive planning. Perhaps if he introduced a part for distant cowbells? Sensitively scored, this pleasing effect would give the piece that extra *something*. No compromise to his artistic integrity either, for didn't Mahler's Seventh Symphony —?

Again he was sure he'd heard his name being called.

He turned for a second time…and *that* was the precise moment when the world all of us had known and cherished – a world arranged for our comfort and security thanks to corporate image-branding, twenty-four-hour news updates, limitless credit facilities and the rest – was changed for ever.

Each of us has our own story to tell: where we were when we heard what had happened, who we were with. TV screens replayed the same terrible image over and over again. We switched them off and still we saw it, burned into our minds. Where it has stayed burned. It was as if the celestial clock, its perpetual *tick-tick-tick* so familiar to us that we no longer heard it – had actually *paused*. Bringing all Creation to a standstill.

Remember?

And then it resumed, in an awkward and unfamiliar rhythm. The hands re-set, it started up again. Since then nothing's felt quite the same.

No need to look very hard to see how things have changed: the sky's been replaced by a Tiepolo-style ceiling of angels gazing down at us, there are chandeliers for sunlight, papier-mâché columns support the weightless architecture of our cities and towns. The streets are clogged with chamber ensembles, the undergrounds with massed choirs. The arms of the violinists ache, the lips of the brass sections are chapped and bleeding, conductors rehearse in their sleep.

Composer Y, at last, is in constant demand. He and his double-bass rush here, there and everywhere, playing to relentless applause. They perform, take their bow and leave. No time to rest, he straps himself to his double-bass, and rushes off. His back bent nearly double, his knees buckling till they almost scrape the pavement, he is determined to keep to schedule. On foot, by bus, taxi, limo, train, ferry, plane and parachute. The next hall, the next concert, the next audience.

Sometimes, exhausted to the very bone, he pauses to gaze up into the stillness of painted clouds and the illusory depth of sky now arching above us all: he draws strength from the wingèd cherubim and seraphim, he stares into the perfectly calculated perspective. There *is* a vanishing-point – and at these moments he can feel it pulling him irresistibly towards nothingness.

When the moment passes, he hurries on. The rest of us, as if fearing to sense even gravity itself as a confirmation of our new loneliness and dread, cheer him louder and louder, clapping and calling for more. Cries of 'Encore!' tear our throats raw.

Composer Z explores the emptiness lying beyond the end of the alphabet

His location at the very end of the alphabet gives Composer Z a sense of being that little bit special: part of the natural order of things, yet close to mysteries that his fellow-composers can only dream of. Lately, he's become more and more drawn to this unexplored domain, often referring to it, in mock suburban-speak, as 'his better half'. This is on good days.

Today's been a bad day. It began with an egg, an egg that rolled. So much for breakfast, he thought, looking down at the mess on the kitchen floor. A small enough event, but ominous. Knowing that entropy is either constant or increasing, and the universe itself perpetually falling apart, Composer Z lives in daily anticipation of his elbows sinking through the table, the floor-tiles disintegrating under his feet. The egg's spontaneous self-destruct said it all.

Just then his wife came through, waving the morning paper: 'They've declared war – a war on terrorism.'

The front page showed the current American president glaring at a collection of foreign-looking heads stuck like stamps down the side of his own nearly full-page photograph. For an instant Composer Z sensed the solidity of the kitchen's laminated worktops and wall units rippling slightly — as if a stone had been flung into the small domestic pool where they lived.

'Plenty of terrorists in Britain. Is he declaring war on us?'

She shook her head. 'No, we're going to be fighting terrorists too, as well as helping to liberate the oppressed.'

He nodded and kissed her. That done, he owned up to the clotted smear of egg yolk, shell and stickiness next to the cooker.

In his study he walked across to the extra-large window he's had installed to give himself a perfect view of whatever lies beyond the end of the alphabet. It is less a scene than an atmosphere, one whose mood changes from day to day: an emptiness that sometimes soothes, sometimes threatens and at other times seems charged with fragility.

Just at that moment, for example, it looked calm and inviting, undisturbed by the clamour of neighbouring composers struggling to make themselves heard. The world — from his morning egg to the President of the USA — might be hurtling towards chaos but here, at least, was refuge from the human din.

He stepped closer and pressed his fingers hard on the glass, like a prisoner gripping the bars. Behind him he could hear the repeated opening and closing of the front door as the members of his wife's chamber group arrived for rehearsal. They greeted each other, he heard the words 'liberation', 'global terrorism', 'eggs', 'omelettes' and 'men'. Then came the tuning up.

Composer Z pressed the plate-glass window even harder and, to his surprise, his fingertips sank into its putty-soft surface.

Within seconds his hands, arms, head, neck and shoulders had slipped through. *Whoa!* he thought to himself. *The next stage in particle disorder, perhaps. But I don't have to go along with it.*

By then, his chest was through and his waist had almost followed. Had his wife shown up at that moment, she would have seen his lower limbs only, executing a distressed wave of farewell.

More half-out the world than in, Composer Z was having seriously to consider his position. And he was failing miserably. Unconstrained by the alphabet, by logic or language in any form, there seemed to be no 'up' out here, or 'down', no 'back', 'forwards' or 'sideways'. What might once have been clouds now prowled what might once have been foreground. What might once have been primary colours seeped into each other and leaked away into what might once have been background.

To keep up his spirits, he whistled the opening bars of his current work-in-progress: a transcription, for strings and percussion, of the genetic coding of the smallest known being on earth. (Waist measurement: 400 millionth of a millimetre.) All at once, like Scottish midges or the dead in Hades – both of which are summoned by human blood – these micro-organisms appeared out of nowhere, answering to their theme tune. Composer Z soon lost count of the millions, billions and trillions crowding around him, getting into his hair, his mouth, his eyes. *What's with this counting?* he thought. He began swatting them. Hopeless, of course. Only when he stopped whistling did they separate, begin to fade and gradually flitter into invisibility. A moment later they were gone.

But he'd got the idea. In quick succession he whistled up The Drunken Sailor, Figaro, the Scottish World Cup Squad and Lili Marlene, and was closing his impromptu concert with a soothing Bach chorale when things started to go very wrong. By themselves, it seemed, the phrases were bending like lines of force, the rhythms stretching, the very notes themselves drifting free of their bar-lines...

Bach's melody was sliding out of reach, soaring far above Composer Z until, quite unexpectedly, it dipped out of sight beyond the shifting horizon – drawing the rest of him after. Pulling him like a cork out of a bottle.

Yes, Composer Z was having a bad day.

His last thoughts, as he shot into nothingness, were of his wife. Where the hell was she?

He cried out: 'Help! Help! HELP!'

Nothing happened.

Why doesn't she leave the Hindemith without even waiting for the next page-turn, and come to his rescue?

He screamed: 'HELP ME! HELP ME! HELP ME!'

Couldn't she hear him?

No, she couldn't. So she didn't come. She didn't rescue him. Not in this universe anyway. In this universe, alas, Composer Z never returned from beyond the end of the alphabet.

Composer Z and his wife are having dinner. Over the Dover sole, broccoli and new potatoes, he tells her about his bad day. He explains the human need to overcome chaos; about human history being man's ongoing attempt to make sense of things by perceiving patterns. But not too much sense, he jokes, or we'll all end up like Linnaeus, in the madhouse. He's paused for her to ask who Linnaeus was.

She doesn't.

Picking up the beat a moment later, he details the hidden agendas of multinationals and the interdependency of business, mass media and government. He lists phrases like *the big players, globalisation, corporate identity*.

Mrs Z has made a special white sauce to accompany the fish.

McDonald's, Monsanto, Exxon, Coca Cola and CNN – he counts them off on his fingers. Imperialism? he asks, then answers: the *Disneyfication* of political truth. The hunt for Bin Laden, Ál-Qa'ida, the liberation of Iraq? – nothing more than the Bambi-face of state terrorism.

His wife interrupts to ask if he has finished.

Though poised to deliver a particularly insightful remark about the stock exchange as a metaphor for...he pauses.

'Well, I'm —'

'The sole, the white sauce, the broccoli, the new potatoes? Finished?'

'Eh? Yes, thanks. I —'

He's paused for her to ask who Linnaeus was

She collects their plates and takes them through to the kitchen, closing the door firmly behind her.

The stock exchange? He'd meant it as a metaphor for…? As he struggles to remember, he hears the clatter of dishes and the rush of tap water.

Alone at the dining-table, Composer Z feels uneasy. He looks across at his wife's empty chair. Despite everything that has happened today, his familiar world of orchestras and chamber groups, presidents and terrorists is still more or less intact, isn't it? He left it and he has returned…no?

Well, hasn't he?

What did he see beyond the end of the alphabet? A breath of wind turning enchanted palaces, fountains of immortality, hospitals, churches and schools into rubble? Houses, streets and marketplaces into blown sand? Everything into desert?

Of course he didn't.

Did he watch elementary particles, like clouds of distant stars, scatter in all directions? Did he see them become…what? Worlds of light and darkness?

Of course not.

Whatever, he knows one thing: that he is now in his rightful place. He is quite sure of that.

He is flesh, blood and bone, with nothing left over. End of story.

The thoughts

David Hume and the pixels of gratification

Having cashed his giro into small change, David Hume, the greatest philosopher of all Scottish Enlightenments past and present, jingled his way into The Stappit Haggis and headed straight for the bar.

'A half-an-half.'

All around were the wasted and damned. On giro-less days he considered them his colleagues in true scepticism, but today his clinking pockets silenced the voice of natural benevolence. As he reached over for his drink, there was a crunch of brittleness from down below, some user lying underfoot. Hume apologised, pulled himself free and found an empty seat on the pub's mock-velvet banquette. He sipped, gazing around the scene of human desolation.

'Right enough,' he remarked to no one in particular.

Two half-an-halfs later he noticed Happy Hour had started. TV blasted one end of the place and techno the other. The place was heaving with MSPs and city councillors, ministers and lawyers, smart money, insurance, property and pensions, plus a detached clump of stunted men in bowler hats with violence in their eyes. The dealers and users resented the lost time and the surrendered space; they glared at these Happy Hour incomers, despising them as clock-watching cheapskates. So did Hume.

'See yous!' he called out.

No less a man than Bertrand Russell had been forced to admit that Hume's masterly refutation of rationality has remained unanswered for the last two hundred and fifty years; likewise in The Stappit Haggis, the jostlers for cheap drink ignored the great philosopher's words. On all sides, propositions of logical inference were being put to the test:

- Drink implies more drink
- More drink implies insufficient drink
- Nothing to drink implies too much
- Enough implies oblivion

Forty minutes into Happy Hour, Hume hauled himself on to his feet to address these heedless critics, 'Proves nothing.'

Having ordered himself another half-an-half, he sat down again – this time moving to a quieter stretch of the banquette, next to Ellen. As usual she was sitting apart – there was the bracing coldness in the air around her, and the mock-velvet had stiffened to ice-hardness. Ellen was a beggar who had come so close to freezing to death on the pavement outside the Caledonian Hotel the previous winter that she had never warmed up again. Her mind remained stuck in permafrost, her social skills reduced to one solitary gesture: the stretching out of her hands in front of her, palms upwards. Either this was to beg or else to offer up all that she was, no one was quite sure which. Some people thought she was a saint, others a complete nuisance. But everyone agreed she was special.

'Hello, Ellen.'

As always, she was wearing the colours that had settled on her that sub-zero afternoon: a cloak-like garment of slate-grey to near darkness, a scarf of winter-dusk shot through with sleet; her skin was ice-blue going on transparent. Whenever she lifted her glass to her lips, it misted over and the surface of her drink froze. But she was enjoying herself; everyone was enjoying themselves during Happy Hour.

'Universal Happiness,' declared Hume, letting the generous sweep of his arm take in the entire bar, the Wee Frees included. He gave them a grin and a thumbs-up, then turned to Ellen. 'Poor sods, believing they're Chosen and that God's domain's The Stappit Haggis!' He shook his head, then, on a moment's impulse, jumped up and scattered fistfuls of five-pence pieces into the air. A scramble began.

His week's giro money, gone. He could relax.

With a sigh he showed Ellen the emptiness now cradled in his own hand: 'I have failed. Failed.' By this time, his series of half-an-halfs had all but cleared away the mists of philosophical scepticism, exposing true bedrock. 'And there's no bedrock like failure, not around here anyroad,' he remarked aloud.

Together they watched the scramble develop, with several MSPs and lawyers in particular showing their skill. Although he was not a religious man, Hume found himself remembering the miracle of Christ feeding the five thousand – had there been a scramble then too? He didn't think so. Or maybe the absence of one was, in itself, the miracle? After all, a few loaves and fishes had fed Scotland for generations. Best to avert his eyes before he saw something he'd regret.

'OK, Ellen?'

Just then a genuine miracle took place.

Had it been his abrupt and careless generosity that jolted her from her trance? Because, quite unexpectedly, Ellen had reached across to place her empty hand in his. Her touch felt ice-cold. Or was it burning? She looked into his eyes, then spoke: 'Please?'

Though her hand, that transparency of flesh and destitution, lay weightless on his own, he seemed unable to withdraw.

'What is it, Ellen?'

From the crash of breaking bar-stools, the splintering of formica tables and the attempts to turn all available art – *The Stag at Bay* and *The Last Chieftain*, plus a conceptual effort that was mostly redefined space – into weaponry, it was clear that the scramble had really caught on. Dealers and users joined in to protect their home-from-home.

But The Stappit Haggis faded far into the distance as Hume leaned closer to catch whatever Ellen might reveal in the moment of her transfiguration. Her hair was almost colourless. Like strands of tangled mist, unwashed, unbrushed and uncared-for, it fell across her face, partly shielding her. Her skin was paper-thin, as if the slightest touch might bruise but hardly draw red blood. Her eyes alone seemed living, glittering now with an unaccustomed and chill light.

'Ellen? What can I do to —?'

Before he could finish, she had laid a finger to his lips to silence him.

In the course of writing about the problems of identity in his *Treatise of Human Nature*, Hume had acknowledged that when he looked into himself he could find only 'a bundle of perceptions', not a 'himself' as distinct from any particular thought, feeling or sense-experience. It was compassion that was now overwhelming him. Like her touch, he felt himself freeze and burn at the same time, and could not let go.

The two of them got to their feet and, together, passed unharmed through the riot of greed and thirst. A few moments later, like ghosts gone astray, they emerged arm-in-arm from the primal swirl of chaos and destruction to step into the real world.

Even at a first glance, it was clear that Edinburgh, the Athens of the North, had been doing its best to keep pace with the times. Life-improvements greeted them on every side: the Festival City was better, faster, more efficient, offering greater choice and guaranteeing instant consumer-satisfaction. The whole urban experience was being constantly updated for their comfort and security. Within seconds, this dizzying rush of progress completed what his several half-an-halfs had begun.

'World's our touch-screen, Ellen,' he slurred. 'Gra'f'cation's all that's left. The pixels of gratification.'

But Ellen seemed hardly to be listening. Coming at a low angle along the Royal Mile the setting sun slanted through her, making her transparency glow from deep within. For several moments a blinding radiance filled the street.

Next thing, Ellen was gone. Vanished completely. David Hume, the sceptics' sceptic, couldn't believe it. He was bewildered. No Ellen. Nothing. Once again he was alone, stranded in this makeshift world put together from the sweepings of history. He gazed around at the abandoned tenements and boarded-up shop windows, at the drabness relieved, here and there, by torn Festival posters and spatterings of Happy Hour vomit. He watched men and women trudge the length of South Bridge, weighed down with special offers at giveaway prices. No one screamed, no one laughed. No one spoke.

Drawing himself to his full height, Hume glared at everyone and everything in sight. He shook his fist: 'See yous! See yous!' He kicked the nearest lamp-post. 'Bus lanes! Dogshite! Parking zones! Bin bags!' before moving on to the nearest fast-food outlet and kicking it. 'Lifestyles! Loyalty cards! Designer labels! Free gifts! Supasavers! Best buys! Must-haves! MUZAK! MUZAK! MUZAK!'

Then he halted, his fist rigid and trembling in mid-shake, his foot poised-and-trembling in mid-kick. For – from behind the diesel-snarls of taxis and double-deckers, from the Cowgate down below, from Princes Street beyond, from the southern slopes of Grange, from the northern gloom and mausoleum-grandeur of the New Town – there had come to him a glorious vision.

Ellen had gone, but all at once he was aware of her presence everywhere around him: a sense of human longing expressed as empty streets and the open sky. The city was dissolving into him, and he into the city.

He stood motionless, letting her humility and grace flow into him.

Was now not the perfect moment to end it all – to give up philosophy and become a paid-up member of society, say, to take his rightful place as citizen and consumer in a well-ordered…?

Just then the Tron Kirk clock coughed its steeple-cough, drew breath and struck the first *Boing!*

Awakened to the danger of his situation, Hume instantly took stock: only seven *boings* remained between him and the end of

Boing!

…Happy Hour. He needed a life plan, and quick.

Boing!

…A menu of career-options conceived, prioritised and processed in

Boing!

…a split-second. A decision-making procedure that would

Boing!

…allow a review of possible strategies for subsequent

Boing!

implementation. Or else, leg it straight back to The Stappit Haggis?

Boing!

…With only one boing left, he knew he'd have to

Boing!

…

Too late. Too late. Too late.

Which meant he now had all the time in the world.

He crossed the street and strolled off down the Royal Mile. He didn't have to do anything. Not anymore, not ever.

Not unless he really wanted to, of course.

Nietzsche breaks through the cycle of eternal recurrence

Nietzsche's chicken farm was a failure. Given his Theory of Eternal Recurrence, he'd been hoping for a nice little earner: chickens-and-eggs, eggs-and-chickens until the end of time — while he dished out the corn and cashed the cheques. But no. All through his teenage years he had stuck at it. While the rest of Sils Maria was out partying, he'd pored over the latest feeding catalogues and roosting charts or passed the evenings hunting for that last egg. He was determined to make it pay.

Then disaster struck. At the age of twenty-three he was appointed Professor of Philology. Even then he didn't give up the hens, despite the endless paperwork, the students, the departmental meetings, the sherry parties. All he wanted was to get on with his series of philosophical masterpieces...and attend to his hen-house. But worse was to come.

Following the publication of *The Birth of Tragedy* he received a faculty memo complimenting him on the brilliance of his work and acknowledging that his increasing academic reputation was adding immeasurably to the university's standing, both at home and abroad. Greater men than he would have heard the alarm bells ringing. But Nietzsche was flattered and touched by the faculty's generous attention. A second memo quickly followed, inviting him to call in at the Admin. block. Greater men than he would have binned it.

'Times are hard,' bleated the basement bean-counters. 'Per capita funding from the government is a help, but you, Herr Professor, are a marketable asset.' They smiled at him. He smiled back. They smiled again. 'Thank you. We knew you would agree. And so, *with* your permission,' and they laughed, 'Or even without it...'

In the pause left for him, the innocent philosopher joined in their laughter and waited to hear what was coming next.

Thanks to the ease of access arising from Switzerland's integrated transport system and the possibilities of cheap ticketing this opened up through group reductions, the *Nietzsche-haus* proved an immediate success. From day one Nietzsche's life was a nightmare. He'd want a favourite pen, his walking stick or the manuscript he'd been writing the previous day – only to find it labelled and locked away behind glass. Even worse, he'd just be settling down to work on the latest Zarathustra episode, say, when his study door would open and in would troop a delegation of visiting Young Hegelians or the Thurgau Women's Epistemological Society. Awkwardly polite, they'd stand at a reverent distance from him, and *watch*. Their discreet shufflings, mutterings and whisperings registered his every quill-scratch or nose-pick; to say the very least, his visitors cramped his prose style. As did having to queue to use his own bathroom.

By the end of the first week Nietzsche had had enough. There was only one thing to be done: the chicken-farm had to be rationalised and its profitability turned around. If he *had* to walk among men, he reasoned, then let it be with a tray of freshly laid eggs for sale.

The following Monday morning his new alarm clock wrenched him from sleep. But he was grateful: its stridency was all that stood between him and a repeat performance, in his jimjams and dressing-gown, of a very public ten-minute wait to get in to shower. He reached for his slippers, then padded off down the corridor. Half an hour later, washed, brushed and breakfasted, he left to gather the morning's eggs.

Walking stick in one hand, egg basket in the other, he stepped out into the spring morning. The sun was shining, the winter snows melting and a fuller spectrum of colour returning to the earth. He rejoiced quietly to himself. On days like this he felt almost at one with his *persona philosophica*, the fictional Zarathustra, breathing deeply the tang of freedom in the mountain air. As he made his way through the village, he was greeted by shop owners, innkeepers, waitresses and chambermaids, all of whom doffed their alpine hats or curtsied, calling out: 'Guten Morgen, Herr Professor.' *Übermensch* or not, Nietzsche was a shy man. To their cheerful hailings he would mutter a response and, if a Heidi lookalike smiled down at him from a balcony, he would blush. How they beamed back at him! They were deeply grateful for the trainloads and coachloads of punters arriving daily to observe the domestic arrangements of their most celebrated citizen. The great philosopher was *their* nice little earner. The university bean-counters had set up a 'Nietzsche Merchandise and Souvenir Shop' and a *wurst* stand in the courtyard, then run out of ideas. Not so the villagers. Most successful of all was an establishment that doubled as the Apollonian Tearoom by day and Club Dionysia by night.

Gradually the houses began thinning out. Ahead lay the Silsersee and, on a wooded promontory jutting out into the stillness of the lake, his hen-house.

The first hint that the cycle of Eternal Recurrence had irretrievably broken came when he heard a *cluck* from high in a nearby tree.

He glanced up. 'Lotte?'

Yes, it was indeed Lotte. Several branches up. Her claws curled securely for balance, she rocked herself backwards and forwards, clucking in full voice. In answer came other *clucks*, unseen and clamouring, from other branches, other trees.

Nietzsche slumped down on the steps of the deserted hen-house. He was desolate. Feathers and pieces of straw whirled around him and, when they settled in his hair and on his clothes, he didn't even bother picking them off. The unlatched door banged every so often like a slow handclap.

Up in her tree, Lotte clenched her claws more tightly around her branch, then stood to her full height to allow herself an open-and-stretch of wings. She preened herself, enjoyed a few satisfying darts and pecks among the spread-out feathers before folding them about her once more. She gazed down at God in his ruined world. How had she ever come to put her trust in one so featherless?

What would Zarathustra do in his place? Nietzsche wondered to himself. All very well for that fictional philosopher living up in the mountains on imaginary berries and spring water, then descending every so often to the level of lesser mortals with the latest bulletin from the moral front...If that naïve, neo-gnostic know-all ever had a hen-house to look after, his message would be very different. Eggs, not ethics, make the best omelettes.

Nietzsche flinched, suddenly appalled at himself. What on earth was he thinking of? Betraying everything he'd ever believed in. Cut them where you will, thoughts like these spelled corruption. Could a lifetime's philosophic integrity be destroyed overnight by a few loose hens and a jerry-built DIY hen-house?

Lotte, meanwhile, was enjoying her day out. From her new alfresco perch she could see across the unruffled sheen of the lake to the mountains. To her, the clouds drifting across the sun looked like a lazily poached egg slithering across its plate of porcelain-blue sky. Hers was a generous world, of corn received and eggs given. The universe was her hen-run. She gave God a second glance. Poor God, she thought. Then enjoyed a peristaltic ripple of her ovary muscles. Soon it would be time to find somewhere dry, warm and secret. She could feel an egg coming on, and hoped it wasn't twins.

For Nietzsche, however, one corrosive thought was leading to the next. A moment earlier, with all the force of a lightning flash, he seemed to have glimpsed the solution. Break up the hen-house, set free the hens, set free himself. He'd been just about to start kicking at the flimsy woodwork when a series of further lightning flashes – each more urgent than the last – struck him. These were propositions that bordered on the axiomatic in their terrifying inevitability:

No hen-house = no eggs
No eggs = no generated income
No generated income = a life doomed to be lived out as an exhibit in his very own museum

Which meant the hen-house had to stay. The hens had to stay. Such was the price-tag of freedom. Then he had the most wonderful idea.

That night as he blew out the candle, Nietzsche knew he was going to sleep the sleep of a man contented. Moonlight and chill air might slip in between gaps in the walls, the occasional star might show through the occasional crack in the badly fitting roof but, as he snuggled himself down in the darkness, he was warm and at peace.

As Zarathustra, he might urge men to grow long legs to step from peak to peak and suchlike extravagances to promote an alertness of spirit, but here, in his hen-house, Nietzsche felt he had 'cracked it'. (Eggs were to be the metaphor of choice from now on.) Unexpectedly at that moment, there popped into his head one of Goethe's more mystical utterances, one that had hitherto baffled him. When shown what lay in the deepest recess of the Abyss, Faust had cried aloud: 'The Mothers! The Mothers!' But, such was Nietzsche's sense of intellectual and spiritual ease just then, that even that enigma now made perfect sense. Rather than a disturbance, the sleepy *clucks* coming from the perches above where he lay duvetted by straw and feathers, had become a soothing chorus of maternity. Whether or not their maternity was cost-effective no longer mattered. Coddled in his nest beneath the surge of the wind and the undeciphered history of the night sky, he felt freer than he had for years, freer and yet more secure.

He drifted down into the shadowland of self, dreaming he was the liberated Zarathustra wandering the upper slopes. From peak to peak he strode, scattering corn as he went, darkening the unmarked snow – with villages, roads, railway lines, the upmarket hotels of St Moritz...

Seneca comes to the Southside

Every so often in his later years Seneca the Stoic found himself considering a move to Edinburgh's Southside. Leaky tenements, student parties, double-parking, Scottish neighbours. Surviving the likes of that would surely secure Stoicism's place, once and for all, as *numero uno* among the world's philosophies.

The day he and his retinue turned into West Newington Place could not have been improved upon. Low cloud covered the stonework like sodden mould; horizontal sleet lashed the aged and infirm on their way to the chemist's at the corner; Pizza Hut cartons, screwed-up chip wrappings and spilled carry-out rice filled the gaps between dogshit.

Seneca's life of ease as the second richest man in ancient Rome was now far behind him – ahead lay the challenge of Scotland in the twenty-first century. He stepped out of his sedan-chair and ordered Nubian Slave I to unlock, then shoulder open, the door of number twelve. His heart rose at the sight of the paint-peeling walls, the strobe-effect stair lighting, the stack of flyers and uncollected mail on the lowest step. He beamed: 'Top flat – and, of course, no lift!'

*

By tea-time he had unpacked and was settled in: canopied bed in the front room, feasting-table and couches in the back, Nubian slaves in the boxroom. Behind a screen the dancing-girls were getting changed into their silks and tassels. Outdoors, the sleet had turned to a greyish snow that became slush the instant it touched pavement. 'Like so much scraped-out porridge,' Seneca observed to himself in a first tentative attempt to take the Scottish viewpoint. He shut the curtains. Cosy. A bowlful of the local wine, suitably warmed, and he'd be ready to resume work on his latest Moral Essay. He'd reached Book IX, 'On Tranquillity of Mind'.

Just then his mobile rang.

When he returned the receiver to Nubian Slave V a few minutes later, it was with a gesture 'weighted with sorrow', as Horace himself might have put it.

'Even here in this barbarian desolation, O Quintus, Destiny marks me with her favour.' The philosopher shook his noble head. 'Though stripped of wealth and all its trappings, I am Chosen. No man can ever know what Fate…'

Quintus, being one of the trappings, stopped listening. Hundred-to-one a 'Stoicism' speech was coming up and he intended getting himself comfortable for the long haul. No shuffling, no smiling, no snoring. He clapped his hands for Scribe I to approach, then put himself into *standby* mode: staring straight ahead, as ready to help his master to dinner as to honourable suicide. He didn't mind which anymore.

Once he got into his stride, Seneca could keep the philosophical one-liners coming for scroll after scroll. Tonight, inspired by the stimulating rigour of his new surroundings, he was quick to hit midseason form and every so often had to pause in his dictation to let Scribe I unroll a further stretch of parchment, re-ink his quill and catch up. As his philosophic stride lengthened, there came, from behind the screen where the dancing-girls waited, the increasingly frequent rustle of silks and shake of tassels. Then the sneezes started. Seneca ignored them, naturally.

*

The downstairs bell rang at 8:30. Thanks to the philosopher's extended peroration no preparations had been made to receive their honoured guest. Less than a minute remained, the time it would take someone to trudge up the four flights from the street. These sixty seconds Seneca devoted to considering whether the audience he was about to grant should be public – in the presence of Nubian slaves, scribes, cooks and dancing-girls – or in camera, with an attendant scribe to video the event for posterity.

The visitor, a man called Murray who'd come all the way from Portobello, was catching his breath halfway up the fourth flight when he heard the sounds of plucked strings and the delicately chimed *ding* that he knew could only be finger cymbals and ankle bells. His first thought was 'drugs'. Not that he cared. Due to the double-parking he'd been forced to leave his car halfway down Causewayside and was soaked through from hatless head to squelchy shoes. He'd be happy to settle for a blast of something himself.

Finally, after hauling himself up the last steps, he found he was expected to ring the bell. To ring the bell, and wait. This really pissed him off. He'd buzzed them on the security panel downstairs, hadn't he? That was four flights ago. Couldn't they tear themselves away from the central heating to be at the door to greet him?

Meanwhile, the dancing-girls had been ordered into the routine that always got an evening with Nero off to a good start: 'Topless on the Tiber' involved a vigorous rowing action that was greatly appreciated by the young emperor. The least they could hope for here was that it might stave off hypothermia. Scribe II was ready to video, the Nubian slaves to prostrate themselves at a given signal. Seneca, modestly toga-ed and sandalled, waited in patrician silence.

When he stepped into the hall, Murray gripped his kitchen-design samples case and stared in all directions at once. His usual opening: 'Good-evening-sir-and-is-this-your-lovely-wife …?' remained unsaid as his gaze followed the chorus-line of topless Tiber-girls up the hall, into the front room and back down again.

Seneca stepped forward. '*Salve, amice!*'

Murray took an even tighter grip of his sample case, and held on.

'Good evening sir, and is this your…?' he managed before falling silent once more.

Seneca gave a magisterial clap of his hands. The Nubian slaves prostrated themselves on the lino and the dancing-girls rustled themselves into a semicircle of honour on the far side of the feasting-table. Scribe II zoomed in to catch every detail of their visitor's entry.

Murray edged forward into the kitchen. 'Have I called at a bad time?'

Having been reassured by his host that all moments in a destined world are equally propitious, he began his customary spiel: laying out the photographs, the sample veneers and mouldings, getting the girls to measure the sink, the cooker, count the sockets, make tea. Involve the customer and they'll feel they've already made an investment in the sale, he had been instructed during that first training weekend. Murray had never really expected to succeed as a salesman, and in this he had anticipated wisely. A month of follow-up calls and he'd sold one set of mixer-taps — mixer-taps that had proved faulty and subsequently been returned. Tonight's pitch would be make-or-break time.

The signs were hopeful. The presence of dancing-girls, Nubian slaves, scribes and cooks suggested a client not stuck for a few bob — a client to be wooed and won. Murray dished out the glossies, the before-and-after pictures, the testimonials from satisfied customers, the coloured charts and statistics on energy-saving. Toga-man was looking a better prospect by the moment. For once, things were shaping up nicely.

While examining the brochures, Seneca reflected on the unexpectedness of such rewards for moral superiority. Deserved or not, these treasures were being given to him, and him alone. As

Murray edged forward into the kitchen:
'Have I called at a bad time?'

he well knew, the fate of lesser men was not his concern and he had once expressed the same in the most pithy terms: 'It is an unending misery to be worried by the misfortunes of others.' The Stoic, he reminded himself, should accept good fortune with the same calmness he withstands sorrow.

For his own part, Murray could hardly believe what was happening. The mark was going for the Full Monty: the Presidential Package. Solid oak with tempered glass doors, gold-plated handles and towel rails, an island with granite work surface. Plus all the extras.

'Sign here, please.' The salesman's voice shook as he pushed the contract across the feasting-table.

Scribe II moved closer to capture the historic event. For Murray the moment seemed to last for ever with Toga-man leaning forwards in slow-motion, remaining poised, pen in hand, over the dotted line. Then he signed. Abruptly, time jerked forward. Then began speeding up. Murray restrained himself from giving the high five and a whoop of triumph. Suddenly life was looking good. From nowhere to the jackpot in one. From zero to Salesman of the Month. To Salesman of the Year. He was dimly aware of the dancing-girls moving into another routine. They were dancing for him.

As he tore off the customer's copy, he remarked that credit facilities were available, but a cheque would be simplest. He made a joke about cash.

'A cheque? Cash? For what?'

'For – for your new kitchen, of course.' He laughed, nervously.

'I have been Chosen.'

'Yes. And it's true. But you have to *buy* the kitchen first, Mr Seneca. Then you go into this month's special draw.'

'*I* have been Chosen.'

Outside, the snow was getting worse. Edinburgh's Southside was rapidly disappearing from view. It was the beginning of the heaviest fall in years: thick heavy flakes tumbled from the darkness on to the double-parked streets below, covering the pavements and communal gardens of Newington. By the time

Murray emerges, the entire city will have been brought to a standstill, with only a few pedestrians tramping and slithering their way among the abandoned buses and cars. Murray will have to walk all the way home to Portobello.

That period of metropolitan calm was still a few hours off when the members of Seneca household began sensing all was not well between the philosopher and his visitor. One by one the dancing-girls shuffled to a stop. They stood in an awkward line and began shivering. Drops of cymbal- and ankle-bell melody trickled off them into the embarrassed silence. Scribe II ceased videoing.

'I tell you, I have been CHOSEN.'

Murray stared down at the contract and considered the 'ifs' that suddenly made up his life:

If he didn't mention the cooling-off period, the company lawyers would do their job and squeeze the money out of Toga-man. Result, his sale would be safe.

If he bent the rules this once, he could look forward to the well-deserved certainty of bending them frequently from now on.

If he failed this time, he failed for good.

Later, having closed the door on the salesman, Seneca stood at the window enjoying a last cup of tea before bed. Stoicism had earned him a new kitchen. In the short-term, at least. There was a cooling-off period about which the salesman had muttered something under his breath, but the philosopher had good ears. He would sleep on it, while trying not to let the unfairness of all things temporal get to him. He was the leading Stoic of the ancient world, wasn't he?

Well, wasn't he?

In years to come Seneca will die by his own hand, falling on to his sword by order of his illustrious pupil Nero. That evening as he stood and watched the snow drift down to cover the city, he repeated over and over to himself, 'I was Chosen, I was Chosen'. It was like anticipating, again and again, the sharpness of his sword as he tests his weight on its tip, before running himself through.

Socrates celebrates the opening of the first supermarket

Part one

Not being one for small talk, Socrates welcomed the opening of the first supermarket in ancient Greece. Years of stopping his fellow-citizens at street corners and in shop doorways to engage them in dialogues about the immortality of the soul – 'Buttonholing folk,' as his detractors described his philosophic method – had made him a shunned figure in downtown Athens. Shunned, and misunderstood. But the opening of the first supermarket would surely change everything. A team of behavioural psychologists would have been commissioned to ensure that the layout, muzak, lighting and product-displays created maximum receptivity in the shopper, whose eye-blink rate would be lowered to near-catatonia. This, Socrates knew, would be the perfect setting for philosophic discourse.

That morning he sneaked out the front door on tip-toe. Not a word to Xantippe. If his wife knew where he was going, it would mean lists, lists and more lists.

Far in the distance the harbour of Piraeus lay shimmering in the heat like a ship at anchor, the white stonework seeming to rise and fall on an invisible tide. Beyond it, the blueness of the sea was indistinguishable from the blueness of sky − blue itself being the absence of colour as in the eyes of a new-born child. The colour of innocence, as of the soul forgetting its immortality. And so on, and so on, and so on…But there was no time for philosophy this morning.

He sighed the sigh of the misunderstood, then rushed off to 'Zealous Hellas'.

For all its illusory nature, the transitory world was a tiring place. The heat and glare of the Attic sun, the city noise, the dust that got everywhere, the sharpness of those small stones that slipped into the sides of his sandals…sensations merely, but on days like today, appearance had the bite of reality. Or maybe he was just getting old. He never got invited to parties any more. The last one, at Agathon's, had been written up by Plato, who described him as jawing on and on till everyone else fell asleep. Yes, his street-cred was at rock-bottom. But all that was about to change.

Fifteen minutes later he entered the main square and began pushing his way through the crowd to get a better view. From chit-chat picked up en route, he gathered that a high priestess from the Delphic Oracle was being charioted in to snip the ceremonial ribbon.

As yet, she hadn't arrived. The local media stood around, the tabloids resting their slate tablets, the broadsheets their tablets of stone, parchment rolls or whatever, at their feet. Beyond the uncut ribbon, the factory-fresh supermarket glittered in the sunlight − a pre-fabricated palace of breeze-blocks, plastic hoardings and glass, fronted by a fleet of micro-chariots tethered in lines. The PR flyers stated that anyone who crossed the threshold, whether freeman or slave, would henceforth be called 'a consumer'. Equality before the check-out. This was the ancient city's wake-up call: 'every ring of the till sounds freedom'. Concept-wise, too, things had moved on since the days when the Delphic Oracle was sited where the god Apollo happened to have once killed a snake. This supermarket had been located only after teams of consultants had conducted income-and-spending-pattern studies in correlation with the very latest in demographic analysis. All to maximise consumer-satisfaction. True democracy.

And what a crowd had turned up! Athenians, Thracians, Spartans, Boetians...men, women and slaves from every corner of the empire. An Aeschyles trilogy was one thing, but you soon saw the gaps on the stone seats, like lost teeth. But not here. After the priestess, there'd be libations, a sacrifice, a celebratory ode, a pronouncement. Then the surge for the shelves.

Whenever his progress through the crowd came to a standstill, Socrates reached up to tap the shoulder of whoever was blocking his view, and began, 'Ah, Meno!' assuming it was Meno, 'since our last chat about the immortality of the soul, a further nine points have occurred to me. Let us consider firstly...' At this, Meno always remembered an urgent appointment, and shifted.

Finally Socrates gained the front row of spectators. Close to the 'Zealous Hellas' building, the Attic sun seemed to shine even more brightly. It was well past noon, the Delphic Sybil was clearly late.

'YOU???!'

At the familiar cut of voice Socrates turned.

'YOU! Of all people! Well, that's a surprise, I must say! A new supermarket, last place I'd have expected to...'

His wife. To think he'd pushed his way across a whole squareful of assorted Greeks and foreigners to end up next to Xantippe. 'Try getting you to go to the shops...Spending my time writing out a list of what to get from where and —'

Socrates had once compared himself to a gadfly stinging complacent citizens into uncomfortable thought. His gadfly – to her buzzsaw. He tried the usual: 'Ah, Xantippe. Since our last chat about the immortality of the soul —'

'Can it, buster! Getting you to wipe your feet when you come in the door would be a start…The number of times I've…Most women have house-slaves to…'

The buzzsaw's further observations were ground to incoherence beneath the rumbling wheels of an approaching stretch-chariot.

The crowd gasped, took a collective step forward and craned a collective neck for a better look. Cigarettes were stubbed out as journalists reached for their tablets and parchments. Socrates was pushed and jostled from behind. He stumbled forward. He fell. Struck his head. Everything went black.

Part two

Socrates has woken to find himself lying in a corner of a windowless room. A half-dozen men and women dressed in yellow 'Zealous Hellas' overalls are chatting to each other, unwrapping chocolate biscuits or spooning their mugs for sunken teabags. One of them is reading out horoscopes. There is a dartboard, a wall-chart of colourful shift-rotas and a series of staff-customer dialogues, with illustrations showing the appropriate smiles:

(Welcoming smile) 'Good morning!'
(Inviting smile) 'Would you like a carrier bag?'
(Sincere smile) 'Have a nice day!'

The table next to the wall is covered with tins of tea, coffee, sugar, powdered milk plus another tin for biscuit-money. An urn is set at constant boil, making the room very hot and steamy. There is a smell which might once have been incense.

Around the prone philosopher is a semicircle of candles that have long ago burned down to blackened stumps; rotted leaves and petals lie trampled into the lino. He sighs sleepily. At once everyone stops chattering, chewing or whatever. They stare across at him. After a few seconds a teenage shelf-stacker – the name tag 'Michael' is clipped to the breast pocket of his nylon overalls –

gets to his feet, wipes any unsightly biscuit crumbs from his mouth, and approaches. He clears his throat and, having taken up position immediately in front of the Father of Western Philosophy, removes a piece of rolled-up parchment from his breast pocket. Reading from the top, he launches into what is clearly a formal address: 'There are many pasts, O Socrates, and this one is yours. Not, alas, the cup of hemlock and the glorious martyrdom to philosophic truth – the "pagan crucifixion", as some commentators have mythologised your last days, basing them upon hearsay tales of a courageous and dignified departure from this life. Not for you the noble piece of PR chronicled so movingly by Plato…'

As Socrates hauls himself up to a sitting position, his customary gambit about the immortality of the soul struggles to find expression. It struggles, and fails. He can already feel himself growing weaker. He coughs, preparing to speak, but all that can be heard is the faintest creak as if some far-off and unimportant door were being pushed to.

Michael continues, 'That you lingered on for over two millennia has been a miracle. Granted. But, to put it frankly, this immortality of yours has also been an embarrassment. An embarrassment to the corporate image of 'Zealous Hellas'. Cluttering up that corner and doing nothing while the rest of humanity got on with things: the collapse of the Greek city states, the decline and fall of the Roman Empire, the Dark Ages, the Renaissance, the Enlightenment, two world wars and, more recently, 9/11.

'As you can see, the votive candles have long since guttered to nothing, the flowers strewn on your shrine have withered…'

Socrates sees mists swirling around him. Has he awoken, only to turn over and sleep for ever? To glimpse this passing world, only to surrender once more to eternal darkness? Already he can hardly make out what is being said. Michael's voice has become no more than vibrations of the steam; and the room itself no more than a place of cloud and shadow.

A door at the back of the staffroom has swung open, letting in the clamour of the supermarket. '…checkout number four. Diana to checkout number four,' comes over the tannoy followed by an urgent demand to 'Remember, shoppers, today we have double bonus-points on some brands of frozen food and disposable nappies...'

There is a rushing sound in Socrates' ears, a dizziness, the hit-and-miss beat of his faltering heart. Speech is beyond him; his breathing labours. He struggles to keep his eyelids from closing ...Through the open doorway he has seen...Yes...Oh, what a consolation in these final moments!...The metaphor of the cave – no longer mere metaphor...A vision...The Realm of Perfect Forms ...The Ideal, opening out before him, bathed in shadowless light, duplicated and stacked in row upon row as far as the eye can see...

His last thought: truly, the gods are compassionate.

The last word

Nadia Boulanger has the last word

Hildegard von Bingen was glad she'd climbed on to the roof of her abbey. A clamber up the narrow staircase, open the little hatch-door – and there she was, in the clear air and sky. Her secret sun-trap. Her sanctuary. Occasionally, she just *had* to get away for some quality time – a slice of cake, a sip of wine and solitude, with her back resting against the small wall at the base of the soaring roof.

Completely by herself at last, she loosened her gown. Far below she could see men, women and children toiling away in the fields. Not her responsibility, for the next half-hour, at any rate. She nibbled, sipped and relaxed. Her greatest responsibility was Music. God had breathed life into man and she, in her own way, returned that breath to Him as hymns of praise. When she sang, she was sure she had God's ear for a brief moment. Oh, blasphemous thought, suitable only for the roof!

The wine finished, she pretended she was in the village tavern and placed the glass upside-down on the tiles next to her. She was ready for a refill. She laughed to herself. If only the novices and nuns could see her now!

Unfortunately, they soon would. She could allow herself only another quarter of an hour at most. She closed her eyes and let the sun soak into her...

It had been more of a nudge than a bump. And it came from very close. Then she felt it again, a kind of *tap-tap* at her side. She looked down.

She must have fallen asleep and rolled against her empty glass. Could have been dangerous. Too much wine for a young abbess! She shook her head and leaned over to slide the glass an arm's length away. Another five minutes, please. She closed her eyes once more.

And, almost immediately, she opened them again. The glass was right at her side – as if she hadn't moved it at all. But she'd not been asleep this time, not even dozing. She hadn't rolled over, hadn't moved a centimetre. It was the glass itself – she could see it now, nudging her, sliding back a little and then nudging her again like some small pet wanting attention. She was about to pick it up when she heard a voice calling to her. A woman's voice that seemed to come from far, far away. A woman she had never met was calling her name...

On her tenth birthday young Elisabeth-Claude Jacquet de la Guerre, as she came to be known, had been blindfolded. She'd come into the dining-room expecting to see the table covered with bon-bons, patisserie and, as a centrepiece, a cake made entirely of chocolate, with BON ANNIVERSAIRE picked out in white chocolate on top. There would be ten candles. That's what she'd been hoping for. Instead, the dining-room table was bare, apart from the usual candelabra in the centre, its candles unlit. Then she was blindfolded.

Two voices: on the left, her father's; on the right, her mother's.

Her father: Elisabeth-Claude, come with us.

Her mother: (Elisabeth could feel a ringed finger through the muslin of her birthday dress) *Ma petite*, your father has something to show you. Something very special.

Elisabeth-Claude's first response was to ask about the chocolate cake and trimmings. She checked herself just in time. Her parents were leading her across the room, bypassing the table on her right. Next, they guided her into the main hall, then through the front door, down a step...and into sudden brightness, with the warmth of the sun on her face. The courtyard? Was she going to be given a pony? From the direction of the main gate she could hear the usual Paris street noises. She was being led further.

Her mother: A step down. Careful.

Into the dimness once more. The smell of wood, of sawdust and shavings, varnish. Her father's workshop.

Her father: Put out your hands.

She stumbled forward like a sleepwalker.

Now sit down.

She could hear the sounds of a chair being placed for her.

Now, lower your hands slowly, bringing them gradually towards you.

Complicated, but she did as she was asked.

Nearly two hours passed before she sat back from the keyboard. Her very own harpsichord, built by her father between other commissions. She was alone now. Sunlight was streaming into the basement workshop. She sat for several seconds longer, listening to the last notes dying away into silence.

Yes, she whispered, I am going to dedicate myself to music, like a nun dedicates herself to God. I'll get married, of course, and have children. That will be love. But music will be something even stronger. She added in a very serious voice: This I vow.

Time to locate the cake. Already she could imagine the thick slice she would soon be enjoying, heavy and black as midnight. She could almost taste it. If she shut her eyes, the chocolate became like darkness, complete darkness, filling her. Or like earth, as if she'd been buried.

Open them quickly! She shivered...and stared around her. Where was she? She had never seen this room before. Someone's bedroom. Lying in the bed was a very, very old lady. With the brightest eyes. Kindness-eyes.

After two days there wasn't much left to burn. Fanny Mendelssohn glanced round the room. The smashed grandfather-clock, its empty casing gaping open like a coffin, stood propped against the wall – it would be next. She'd used up all the chairs, the table-legs, then the table itself. The bed. The books. Maybe it was time to start on her songs. Everyone said they were beautiful. Probably they would burn well.

This would be her last fire. One final defiant blaze and she'd be ready to go back downstairs. Go back for the family's appreciation and their polite applause.

Of course her songs would burn well. They were *very* good songs. Even her brother Felix said so – and everyone knew what a genius *he* was. They were good enough to be published – under *his* name.

Everyone in the family said it was for the best. The best for her, the best for them.

Having dismembered the clock, and twisted the music-sheets into kindling, she lit the small pyre. Things were soon blazing nicely.

'Come out of there, Fanny.' Someone was banging on the door. 'Go away!'

Her voice sounded splinter-dry with the smoke. The flames were yellow, red, scarlet. She reached forward to touch their flittering brightness.

The flames settled on her hands like jewels, flashing and swirling over her palms, around her fingers and wrists, glittering with light. There was no pain.

Decked in these brilliant colours she stepped into the fire.

*

It had been raining for days, weeks, months, years. Clara Schumann had got used to living in a city where curtains of water opened and closed, revealing day and night. The streets were raging torrents, waterfalls and dams, the public squares were shallows or flooded deltas. Some homes had become shaded streams, others stagnant ponds, whirlpools, cascades.

For the last few years she had managed to keep poor Robert and her children from drowning, but more recently had felt too exhausted to struggle any longer.

When she went outdoors this morning the waves were lapping at her feet. Caressing her, almost. Their touch felt less like water than purest light. Within moments she was being borne weightlessly forward. The houses on either side seemed to pour themselves into the deeps beneath her. Even when she felt herself letting go and sinking below the surface, she knew there was no danger.

Not any more. No struggle, no exhaustion – only the current carrying her safely, as if in its arms...

Nadia Boulanger has woken to see her dead sister standing at the foot of her bed. Lili, just as she saw her last: twenty-four years old, short black hair, neat dress, her face serious as a child's. She is holding her finger to her lips for silence.

Lili: Don't be afraid. There's only a very short time left, so I've come to welcome you.

Nadia would like to reach out to touch her, but cannot. All her strength has gone.

Lili: And I've invited some others to join us for these last moments.

It's 22nd October 1979. At the age of ninety-two Nadia Boulanger, the greatest teacher of composition in the history of Western music, is on her deathbed. Outside in the Rue Ballu the early evening traffic is a muffled rumble of cars, taxis and buses. Relatives and close friends are gathered in her room – but already they are growing insubstantial, their outlines fading to shifting sunlight and shadow. Meanwhile, Lili and the four other women composers have become quite clear and distinct to her.

Nadia: Mozart and his wife sang parts of his unfinished Requiem on *his* deathbed. That's a pretty hard act to follow.

Hildegard lightly smoothes Nadia's brow with her fingertips. Elisabeth-Claude is stroking the back of her left hand, Fanny has taken her right. From the foot of the bed Clara looks on in silence.

Nadia: Don't look so sad, Clara.

Can the living hear her? Does the doctor think she's delirious? That *smother-rustle* must be her relatives whispering among themselves. Everything that can be done has been done, they'll be reassuring each other.

Nadia: Beethoven died during a storm. After a tremendous crash of thunder he's supposed to have sat bolt-upright in bed and shaken his fist at the heavens, as if raging against Fate to the very last. Then fallen back, dead. That's another hard act to follow.

The shadows of friends and relatives have become still. All conversation ceases.

Nadia: My passing's going to be so very dull. Rush-hour traffic noise, an ordinary Paris flat. The doctor, the friends and relatives – like any of a dozen Balzac death-scenes, but without the intrigue over the will. No drama.

Lili: Do you want drama?

They might.

But do you?

A little, maybe. So that it's something more than just a battery running down. Then coming to a dead stop. As you might say.

Clara: Hmm.

The doctor glances over in the direction of the *hmm*, but can see nothing. Maybe he imagined it. A touch of stage-fright? This is his big moment, after all: he was about to give his professional sad shake-of-the-head to indicate that the end was very near. But that unexpected and unaccountable *hmm* has rather put him off his stroke. It's very hot in the room; he wants to undo his tie and ease open a couple of top buttons. He stops himself in time: he knows the gesture makes him look too much like a car mechanic. Instead, he gives an almost soundless cough – to recover his timing, as it were – then steps back from the patient. Turning away in regret to acknowledge that, in the face of man's mortality, even his skill can do nothing more. Now follows the practised shake of the head.

Lili: We could do some poltergeist stuff, if you want. Pull the curtains open and closed to show your spirit leaving out of the window.

Elisabeth-Claude: Or play the piano – like it was playing itself.

Hildegard: Maybe we could sing together. Like a chorus calling you from the other world.

Nadia: I like the piano idea. I can imagine the write-up: at the moment of her death, Nadia Boulanger's piano sounded out a final lament!

She was now aware of the shadow-people coming up one by one to kiss her, to murmur their parting words.

Nadia: They're saying goodbye. But really it's them that's leaving – not me. Afterwards they'll go out of the flat, back to their homes, their families and their lives. Off into the future. It's me that's staying.

Lili: Staying with us.

As discreetly as he can, the doctor closes his bag. Putting away my tools, he thinks to himself. He's given way and finally loosened the tie ever so slightly and undone the top button. My mechanic's tools, no longer needed as the machine is beyond repair. He withdraws to the window to look down into the street. Darkness is falling: that pause between evening and night which, like four in the morning, is unable to conceal the underlying sadness of human existence.

But, he reminds himself, he's getting married in a week. He's excited. In exactly seven days he'll be at his wedding dinner. His new wife at his side, champagne, his family's happiness and his own. For the moment he has quite forgotten his dying patient.

Nadia: No poltergeist drama, please. As it is, one life is enough of an impossibility and a miracle. Come closer. It's time to take me with you.

Hold me. With your help everything around me and inside me will vanish. Like magic. Like one miracle leading to the next.

Notes about the composers and philosophers

JOHANN SEBASTIAN BACH (1685–1750) wouldn't have needed a computer. He himself was perfectly capable of doing everything the most modern 512 MB PC2100, 120GB HD, 56K modem, with or without DVD, can do, only better – and all the while creating music as close to the celestial harmony of the spheres as any human being could, before becoming divine.

As a young man he did indeed walk two hundred kilometres to hear Buxtehude play. Which almost cost him his job because he walked all the way back as well, arriving too late to play the organ at Sunday church. Several months too late. His children, the Initials, became much better-known musicians than himself. CPE was at the cutting edge of the avant-garde, JC was the darling of London society and also a friend to the seven-year-old Mozart, who visited the city as an infant prodigy. Poor WF was perhaps the most gifted of the three. He was also the eldest. In time he became an alcoholic and ended his days playing for a pittance in dance bands. Such of his music as has survived is quite extraordinary and well worth seeking out.

Knowing death was fast approaching, Bach abandoned the Art

of Fugue. In the already fearsomely complex score he introduced the notes B-A-C-H (in German usage B flat is called B, and B natural is called H), as though putting his signature to what had been written so far. The music breaks off at this point and he died shortly after. In a performance of this miraculous work we have the sense of the series of solitary closing notes reaching out into eternity.

LUDWIG VAN BEETHOVEN (1770–1827) never visited Edinburgh, though he often dreamed about it. The city was his El Dorado. Having been commissioned by George Thomson of Edinburgh to write settings of Scottish folk-songs, he had cleaned up in a big way. As had Haydn. 'These songs are my pension,' said Haydn, rubbing his hands each time he nipped out to cash that week's postal order from Scotland.

Unlike Mozart, Beethoven was one of the first freelance artists to survive. He took the whip hand – driving hard bargains, selling the same piece several times over – and recognised that publishers *needed* composers or they would go out of business. A healthy attitude.

MAXI THE TAXI, of course, still lives in Edinburgh. His numbers increase the further north one goes.

HILDEGARD VON BINGEN (1098–1179) was the most important and, possibly, the sole woman composer of sacred music in the Middle Ages. Not only was she the abbess of a convent, she was also a teacher, a mystic, a writer of visionary and scientific works, and an advisor to heads of state.

Almost as tragic an early death as Mozart's was that of LILI BOULANGER (1893–1918). At twenty-two, she was the only woman composer ever to be awarded the Prix de Rome – the one solitary woman in the prize's one-hundred-year history. Two years later she died. For a hint of the greatness that might have been to come, check out her magnificent setting of Psalm 130.

For nearly seventy years NADIA BOULANGER (1887–1979) was the greatest-ever teacher of music composition. From her correspondence course 'Everything You Need To Know About Composing Contemporary Music', to the better known one-to-one sessions held in her Paris flat, she rescued many a hapless student from enthralment to the Second Viennese School. She put three generations of composers on the musical map, planting them like little flags across Europe and America to mark the victories of Modernism over all other -isms.

JOHANNES BRAHMS (1833–97) started well, then got stuck. Simple as that. In his early years he was 'adopted', in the artistic sense, by the Schumann household. Confident that the first symphony *he* wrote was going to be the 'biggie' after Beethoven's Choral Symphony, he gave himself writer's block, in a big way. Many of his conversations over the next twenty years must have gone like this:

Citizen of Hamburg: Hello, Brahms. How's your first symphony going?

Brahms: Don't ask.

We can only conclude that his sense of historical self-importance finally wore itself out. The symphony, with its magnificent Introduction – a last-minute addition – was written. Then Brahms was able to move on.

COMPOSERS Q, X, Y and Z all live in Edinburgh. Every so often they meet over a few beers to discuss the rest of the alphabet.

Like motorists with car registrations, they look forward to each new year's new letters.

Now that Composer Z has moved into a parallel universe, or something similar, set in Edinburgh's Southside, the others keep an empty chair for him. Sometimes they fancy they can hear his voice droning on about why the world's in such a terrible state. Then they move to another table.

ANTONIN DVOŘÁK (1841–1904) was Bohemian. Towards the end of the nineteenth century, the Hohenzollern, the Habsburgs and the Romanovs were stumbling through the last years of their history, like three drunks propping each other up on the road home. With the collapse of these empires clearly imminent, nationalism broke out like a rash across Europe. Bohemia was only one of several countries where a sudden interest was taken in native folk-songs, dances and stories. The search for national identity was on, and Dvořák was in the forefront with his use of traditional dance forms, like the *dumka*, and his symphonic tone poems based on Bohemian legends.

The composer was a very down-to-earth man – a keen pigeon-fancier and train-spotter. During a trip to America once, he went for a wander round some of New York's train sheds to tick off locomotives not currently in service, and was arrested on suspicion of being a spy. By all accounts he was a kindly, family man.

On the surface, JOSEPH HAYDN (1732–1809) lived an uneventful life. For nearly fifty years he was *Kapellmeister* to the Esterházy family, passing most of each year in the family palace built in the middle of the Hungarian marshes. This splendid isolation allowed him to explore his own creativity free from the distractions of musical fashion. In the event, thanks to Europe being pretty much awash with pirated editions of his works, he himself was the trend-setter, the label to die for.

He produced quantity as well as quality. Possibly one of the most innovative composers ever. Even in the most conventional forms (like the string quartet, which he pioneered) there is always something new to be discovered, a daring harmony, a thrilling development section. But, unlike his pupil Beethoven, he was no revolutionary. This, it must be remembered, was a period of history when lords and ladies were easily alarmed; even the sound of tumbrel wheels on cobbles was enough to set them panicking.

In essence, Haydn was a servant and treated as such; he was expected to produce symphonies, much in the same way as the cook produced dinners, and the artist family portraits.

Unfortunately, his wife hadn't the slightest love of music. Haydn is reported as saying that she was no more interested in his work than if he'd been a cobbler.

From early on, DAVID HUME (1711–76) described his aim in life to be 'the love of literary fame'. The careers officer who suggested he become a philosopher, therefore, would seem to have been a man with a particularly warped sense of humour.

As Hume himself put it, his *Treatise of Human Nature* 'fell dead-born from the press'. He revised it by leaving out the best bits, then republished it under the title *Inquiry Into Human Understanding*. This fared little better. Kant, who seems to have been the only person to read it, announced that it 'woke him from his dogmatic slumbers'. Unfortunately the rest of the Enlightenment wasn't the least bit interested.

When Hume applied for a job as Professor of Philosophy at Edinburgh University, he was turned down. The present multi-storey block of cement which houses many university departments, including that of philosophy, is named after him. The David Hume Tower stands in the bottom right-hand corner of what was once an elegant Georgian square. The modern university turned that down too, with bulldozers and demolition balls, three sides of it, at any rate. Presumably they preferred glass-and-breeze-block neo-brutalism. No wonder Hume doubted pretty much everything, his own self included.

As well as having a most delightful name, ELISABETH-CLAUDE JACQUET DE LA GUERRE (1664–1727) was the first (known) woman composer of instrumental music. From childhood she played the harpsichord (her father really was a harpsichord maker) and, in time, she composed not only for her own instrument, but wrote large-scale pieces for major theatrical events, including opera.

ALMA MAHLER (1879–1964) was told by her husband Gustav that there was room in the family for only one composer, and it wasn't going to be her. After Gustav's death, having 'done' music, she completed collecting her set of 'Artistic Men', by becoming, in turn, the mistress of Oskar Kokoshka the painter, Walter Gropius the architect and the poet Franz Werfel. Known as 'The Widow of the Four Arts' she was reckoned to be one of the great femme fatales.

When she broke off her relationship with Kokoshka, the artist ordered a mannequin to be made in her image. This full-sized Alma doll then accompanied him to parties and bohemian get-togethers. During what was described as 'an orgiastic revel' the doll was beheaded and thrown out of a top-storey window. The headless body became the subject of police enquiries.

FANNY MENDELSSOHN (1805–47) was the sister of Felix, the well-known composer. The available evidence suggests that she had a major talent for music. Unfortunately, she also had a family who knew what was best for her. The society they moved in agreed that, as a woman, Fanny's life was really not her own.

The 'MIGHTY HANDFUL' is one of the first examples of image-branding. In an article written in 1867, the critic Vladimir Stasov grouped five Russian composers together, believing they were creating music that was distinctly nationalistic, in contrast to the European mainstream dominated by the German tradition. But, by and large, the five were their own worst enemies.

MILY BALAKIREV (1837–1910), the founder of the nationalist approach, set up the Free School of Music. As many teachers do, he became disillusioned; feeling he had been defeated by 'official' musicians, he took a minor post in the railways and retired into religious mysticism.

ALEXANDER BORODIN (1833–87) was a family man and a professor of chemistry. To him, music was a hobby.

CÉSAR CUI (1835–1918), was a lightweight, a critic who wrote splenetic articles attacking anyone more famous and more successful than himself. This, as can be imagined, kept him pretty busy. Rather a touching character really, like an adolescent stuck for ever at 'the world's so big and I'm so small' stage. Perhaps this is why, in the story, he's not yet grasped the fact that mortality is something to be taken personally.

MODEST MUSSORGSKY (1839–1881) was crushed between his opera *Boris Godunov*, which he worked on throughout his life and never finished, on the one side, and vodka on the other. In the end, it was the vodka that finished *him*.

NICOLAI RIMSKY-KORSAKOV (1844–1908) came from a naval family and started his career as a sailor. Settling on dry land, he turned to music and never changed course thereafter. He composed not only his own works, but everyone else's too. His motto was: 'If it doesn't move, orchestrate it!'

As the first bicycle was not straddled until 1840 – by its inventor, the Scotsman Kirkpatrick Macmillan who lived near Dumfries – it is unlikely that WOLFGANG AMADEUS MOZART (1756–91) ever learned to ride one. Bearing in mind, however, that the bicycle is regarded by scientists as the most efficient machine ever devised (in terms of work input–output), Mozart would have been a natural. The notion of his mastering aerial cycling is, therefore, not unreasonable.

He played the viola, his favourite instrument, in playing-for-fun quartets on Sunday afternoons with three other major composers of the day, Haydn, Vanhal and Ditters (latterly, von Dittersdorf), at the home of Baron van Swieten, the diplomat. Ah, those were the days.

FRIEDRICH NIETZSCHE (1844–1900) was an intellectual prodigy. Before he had even completed his university degree, he was offered a professorship. Essentially, he was a bookish don with an amazing imagination, plus a stock-in-trade of arresting images. His language is vigorous, passionate and yet elegant – a rare feat in any philosophy, German philosophy in particular.

Primarily, he saw himself as giving the wake-up call to a complacent society sinking into bourgeois torpor and decadence. He was a day-dreamer, a poet: a visionary whose non-systematic philosophy could embrace any and all contradictions. His bedroom at the *Nietzsche-haus* at Sils Maria is like a child's, but very neat and with no toys.

He is best-known for having been hijacked by the Nazis. What an irony – from the bottom of his heart he would have despised every last one of them.

In an attempt to rouse men to a condition of exalted awareness, he urged them to 'pitch their tents on the slopes of Vesuvius'. Hen-houses would have done just as well. In theory, at least.

The *Andantino* movement of FRANZ SCHUBERT's (1797–1828) Piano Sonata in A D959 says it all. The waltz rhythm with its explosive central section seems like a self-portrait: an unassuming and easy-going outer amiability that conceals volcanic incandescence at its core.

At the age of seventeen he became a teacher in his father's school. A couple of years later he did what many teachers would dearly love to do – walked out and never went back. After that he made no compromises with his decision to live by his compositions (he was not a good enough pianist to give solo concerts) and he threw himself into the low-income thrills and spills of the artistic/bohemian life. He fell in love but could not afford to marry, and the poor girl couldn't afford to wait. Hence his bachelor life of thinking and drinking – and Schubertiads. These were evenings of fun and games, drinking, dancing and music-making, poetry reading and friendship, and more drinking.

Masterpiece after masterpiece was created, and ignored. He never heard a single note of many of his large-scale works – including several operas, his best-known symphonies and settings of the mass. When he did get published he got ripped off, thanks to contracts that would have present-day vampires, or even publishers, blushing for shame. Well, they managed to kill the poor man off eventually. But who remembers Diabelli, or any of his music?

By all accounts ROBERT SCHUMANN (1810–56) was a man of wild enthusiasms and crippling despairs. Today he would have been drugged and therapised into a semblance of what passes for acceptable behaviour. Which would probably have made life easier for his family, his colleagues and also for himself. This man really suffered. Was his music the richer for his delusions (that the orchestra he conducted always played too fast, so he had to keep slowing it down, usually to near-standstill) and his paranoia (resulting in various failed attempts at suicide)? Who can tell?

Clara's father certainly saw him, in future-son-in-law terms, as a complete non-starter. Herr Wieck had his own agenda, of course, having constructed Clara along the lines of a concert-machine whereby the Wiecks would make their fortune. He probably also saw the truth of the matter: that musical geniuses don't necessarily make the best husbands. In the event, it was Clara's energy, enterprise and earnings that were to hold the Schumann family together.

Schumann's violin concerto was suppressed by Clara and Joseph Joachim, the famous violinist, who both regarded it as 'poor stuff'. Certainly it was not the usual crowd-pulling *bravura* fodder. The first movement is particularly moving: in it we can hear Schumann's sense of terrible isolation and his struggle to hold a disintegrating world together. If there is a Supreme Being out there, he must be deaf not to have been moved by the man's despair. Not long after completing this work, Schumann was committed to an asylum where he died insane two years later.

An interesting footnote. The concerto might have remained unknown to this day had not the violinist Jelly d'Aranyi, Joachim's great-niece, claimed to have received a message from the composer during a séance, asking her to seek it out.

LUCIUS ANNAEUS SENECA (c.3 BC–65 AD) was born and brought up in Spain. His house – and very nice it is, too – can still be seen in Córdoba. In time, he became Nero's tutor and amassed vast wealth: estimated at three hundred million sesterces (in the modern world, this would have made him a millionaire many, many times over). Not by teaching Nero, of course – but by money-lending. Apparently one of the reasons for the Britons' tendencies to revolt was the excessive rates of interest they were being charged by the philosopher. Uneasy parallels here with contemporary attitudes to Third World debt.

He was a Stoic. His letters were certainly written with an eye to posterity. When committing suicide on the orders of former pupil Nero, he ensured that his closing speech was taken down by a scribe. Instructed to speed things along, Seneca delivered his dying words: 'What I leave you is of far more value than earthly riches, the example of a virtuous life.' Way to go, Lucius Annaeus!

JEAN SIBELIUS (1865–1957) was a perfectionist. And a warning to anyone who thinks perfectionism is the way forward. Becoming more and more self-critical as he grew older, he took longer and longer to finish his works. His symphonies became increasingly condensed until the Seventh; this, the shortest, comes in one unbroken melodic flow. The Eighth was written and rewritten. One movement was actually sent to the printers, then withdrawn. It is assumed that he destroyed all his work on the symphony – nothing of it has ever been found, not even the briefest sketch.

To SOCRATES (c.470–399 BC) the art of conversation was simplicity itself: just keep talking. For the sake of variety, he'd feed his straight man an occasional line needing no more than a 'yes', a 'no' or (even better) a mere nod in reply. He refused all payment for teaching philosophy, believing it would limit his freedom to follow wherever the arguments led.

Central to his philosophy is the image of the cave. Here mankind sits in near-darkness, watching shadows passing along the wall, and taking them for real. Mankind accepts the cave as the only reality. When someone – a true philosopher, of course – struggles free and escapes to the outside, he will see the sun in the sky and *real* things, not their shadows. When he returns with the good news, he will naturally be lynched for attempting to disturb the status quo.

Things haven't changed very much in the last two thousand years.

The jury's still out concerning the degree to which RICHARD STRAUSS (1864–1949) went along with the full Nazi doctrine. He was a party member, but so was anyone else who wanted a job. At that time, choosing to work with the writer Stefan Zweig, who was Jewish, was indeed courageous. In protest at the Nazis' treatment of Zweig he resigned as president of the Reichsmusikkammer. The following year he wrote music for the Berlin Olympic Games. A complex man.

Home life was very much life under the Pauline jackboot. Rumour has it that the fourth doormat in their household was the composer himself.

His inner life, and how he saw himself, can perhaps be illustrated by the title he gave to his autobiographical tone poem of 1899: *Ein Heldenleben* (*A Hero's Life*). Much later, when the Americans turned up at his front door to liberate him at the close of WW2, he greeted them thus: 'I am the world-famous composer, Richard Strauss. You can't shoot me!' Or words to that effect. Still, better safe than sorry. Even with the best of intentions, acts of liberation can so easily end badly.

Being gay, PYOTR ILYCH TCHAIKOVSKY (1840–1893) was very much the wrong sort of man in the wrong place at the wrong time. Nineteenth-century Czarist Russia was not a society that welcomed manly affections, except under the guise of duelling, gambling and drinking. His marriage to Antonina Milyukova, who seems to have been completely off her head, made matters even worse. In less than a month he ran away from the unfortunate woman, and tried to kill himself. By contrast, his relationship with his patroness, the widow Countess Von Meck, must have been heaven-sent. Though she insisted they never meet face-to-face, the two of them corresponded frequently and with a surprising openness. She gave him a generous allowance which freed him from financial worries.

A happy ending? No chance. Tchaikovsky died after he had drunk, quite knowingly, a glass of unboiled water during a cholera epidemic. There is a theory that he did this under duress

– having been ordered to commit suicide as punishment for a sexual indiscretion involving the teenage son of an aristocrat.

Unlike most great composers, GEORG PHILIPP TELEMANN (1681–1767) was also a great businessman. A self-made man and self-taught musician, he founded *Der Getreue Musikmeister* (*The True Music-Master*) to publish and distribute his own works. And very successful it was, too. To get a complete sonata, a flautist for example, would have to buy three consecutive numbers of the magazine. Of course, the third issue also contained the first movement of yet another flute sonata. And so on, and so on. Smart man.

In his day Telemann was the best-known composer in all Europe with ten pages devoted to him in a contemporary *Who's Who in Modern Music*, as opposed to the two-and-a-half lines devoted to a provincial organ-player called J. S. Bach.

As if to balance things, Telemann is very much neglected by the modern world. He most resembles an overgrown garden: over forty-five operas, twelve complete cycles of cantatas for the liturgical year, around fifty settings of the Passion, vast quantities of *Tafelmusik* (music-to-eat-by, a form of very upmarket *muzak*), hundreds of concertos, orchestral suites, trio sonatas, other orchestral and keyboard music. Problem is – just where do you start?

ANTONIO VIVALDI (1678–1741) really did write well over 500 concertos, but only someone with cloth-ears would agree with Stravinsky's assessment. Vivaldi was in poor health for most of his life, and pleaded asthma to avoid his priestly duties. He lived with two sisters, who acted as nurse and housekeeper. There was talk. But hey, what's new? All his passion went into his music. Of course it did.

As the Venice canals were constantly being blocked by the

bodies of abandoned infants, the local council had set up charitable foundling homes like the Pietà, where the children were educated, particularly in music. Thus, in adult life, the girls could gain a livelihood and a husband. Judging from Vivaldi's concertos, they must have been superb musicians, superbly taught.

Other Serpent's Tail titles of interest

Haunted Weather: Music, Silence, and Memory
David Toop

Is it possible to grow electronic sounds, as if they were plants in a garden? Can the resonance of an empty room be played like a musical instrument? Why are childhood memories of sound and silence so important to our emotional development? Is it valid to classify audio recordings of wind or electrical hum as musical compositions? Can computers replace more conventional instruments like the piano or the electric guitar? How can improvisation coexist with computer software? Why have the sounds of our environment become so important to sound artists and why is atmosphere so important in music?

In *Haunted Weather*, David Toop asks these questions and gauges the impact of new technology on contemporary music. Partly personal memoir, partly travel journal, the book explores ways in which the body survives and redefines its boundaries in a period of intense, unsettling change and disembodiment. At the heart of the book is how sound and silence in space, in memory and in the action of performance acquire meaning. *Haunted Weather* is a book that maps 21st century sound as *Ocean of Sound* mapped the sound of the 20th century.

Ocean of Sound: Aether Talk,
Ambient Sound and Imaginary Worlds
David Toop

Sun Ra, Brian Eno, Lee Perry, Kate Bush, Kraftwerk, Aphex Twin,
Ryuichi Sakamoto and Brian Wilson are interviewed in this
extraordinary work of sonic history that travels from the rainforests
of Amazonas to virtual Las Vegas, from David Lynch's dream house,
high in the Hollywood Hills to the megalopolis of Tokyo.

Ocean of Sound begins in 1889 at the Paris Exposition when
Debussy first heard Javanese music performed. An ethereal
culture developed in response to the intangibility of 20th century
communications.

'An erudite and entertaining chauffeur, Toop, a noted ambient
musician himself, shows us a way of listening differently. He
teaches us to enjoy the environmental sounds of pneumatic drills,
police helicopters, and tree frogs. He tells us to appreciate the
silence between the sounds…*Ocean of Sound* puts Toop up there
with Eno as a theorist of ambient music' *Wired*

'David Toop has written a music book which finds common
space for Albert Ayler, Stockhausen, The Orb, Charlie Parker,
William Burroughs, The Future Sound of London, Frank Sinatra,
the Venezuelan Yuekuana Indians and U2. You could call it
stimulating and brilliant – and you'd be right' *Hot Press*

'Overall, this is a hugely optimistic book. When music writers
fish in esoteric pools of anthropology and literature, as Toop does

extensively here, it is often a sign that their original feeding ground is waning. But for all talk of scents and shades, perfumes and tints, it is the capacity of sound to thrill the senses that comes across most clearly in these pages. Dive into *Ocean of Sound* too recklessly and there is a slight risk of drowning, but let it lie around the house a while and it will seep into your brain by osmosis' *Independent on Sunday*

'*Ocean of Sound* brilliantly elaborates both these processes, like sonic fact for our sci-fi present, a Martian Chronicle from this Planet Earth' *The Face*

'A rare instance of a music book which is about music, but works' *Sunday Times*

Exotica: Fabricated Soundscapes in a Real World
David Toop

'To put it starkly, Toop knows far more, about a far broader range of music, than any other critic' *New Statesman*

'Toop is required listening, reading and thinking for anyone with even the remotest interest in the world' *Top Magazine*

What is the exotic? And why does it have such appeal?

David Toop's narrative leaves no tone unheard in its exploration. Merging anecdote and biography, autobiography and interviews, fact and fiction and, of course, a characteristically eclectic selection of music, David Toop spirals us through the 20th century's guilty fascination with exotica. Josephine Baker and Carmen Miranda, schlock sci-fi and shrunken heads, leopard-skin leotards and pink fluffy cubicles, The Modern Jazz Quartet and near-naked Trobriand Islanders freezing in the torrential London rain all feature in this extraordinary, syncopated search through dense imaginary landscapes of the unknown.

Includes interviews with Burt Bacharach, Ornette Coleman, Bill Laswell, YMO's Haroumi Hosono, Nusrat Fateh Ali Khan, The Boo-Yah T.R.I.B.E.

David Toop brings together the words, images and sounds of an extraordinary moment in the culture. Like its predecessor, *Ocean of Sound*, *Exotica* changes the way we hear.